SIMON OF CYRENE:
THE CROSS-BEARER'S LEGACY

SIMON OF CYRENE:
THE CROSS-BEARER'S LEGACY

A Story of the Faith and the Trials of Early Christians

RICHARD NEFF

WestBow
PRESS
A DIVISION OF THOMAS NELSON

The Scripture quotations contained herein are from the New Revised Standard Version Bible, copyright 1989, by the Division of Christian Education of the National Council of the Churches of Christ in the U.S.A. Used by permission. All rights reserved.

WestBow Press books may be ordered through booksellers or by contacting:

WestBow Press
A Division of Thomas Nelson
1663 Liberty Drive
Bloomington, IN 47403
www.westbowpress.com
1-(866) 928-1240

Because of the dynamic nature of the Internet, any web addresses or links contained in this book may have changed since publication and may no longer be valid. The views expressed in this work are solely those of the author and do not necessarily reflect the views of the publisher, and the publisher hereby disclaims any responsibility for them.

Any people depicted in stock imagery provided by Thinkstock are models, and such images are being used for illustrative purposes only.

Certain stock imagery © Thinkstock.

ISBN: 978-1-4497-9519-1 (sc)
ISBN: 978-1-4497-9518-4 (hc)
ISBN: 978-1-4497-9520-7 (e)

Library of Congress Control Number: 2013909003

Printed in the United States of America.

WestBow Press rev. date: 06/18/2013

Dedicated to the memory of my parents

Harry Myer Neff (1899-1993)

and

Ada Sue Baxter Neff (1903-1995)

TABLE OF CONTENTS

INTRODUCTION

My wife has told our grandchildren that there are three kinds of stories. There are stories that happened; we call these stories history, biography, and autobiography. There are stories that did not happen; novels, fairytales, and myths make up this category. And finally, there are stories based on some historical facts that are blended with details that could have happened but are not supported by historical records; these are historical novels.

The story told on the pages that follow is designed as a historical novel, but admittedly it is more novel than history. Perhaps the better term is historical fiction. It is constructed based on a few verses in the New Testament, but much of it flows from my imagination. It could have happened, but there is no evidence it happened the way I have told the story.

The passages from the New Testament that provide the basis for this story are six verses taken from the Gospel according to Mark, the Acts of the Apostles, and Paul's letter to the Romans. These Bible verses are:

> They compelled a passer-by, who was coming in from the country, to carry his cross; it was Simon of Cyrene, the father of Alexander and Rufus. (Mark 15:21)

> Phrygia and Pamphylia, Egypt and parts of Libya belonging to Cyrene . . . (Acts 2:10, listing the countries and areas that were home to the Jewish pilgrims who were in Jerusalem on the Day of Pentecost)

But among them were some men of Cyprus and Cyrene who, on coming to Antioch, spoke to the Hellenists also, proclaiming the Lord Jesus. (Acts 11:20)

Now in the church at Antioch there were prophets and teachers: Barnabas, Simeon who was called Niger, Lucius of Cyrene, Manaen a member of the court of Herod the ruler, and Saul. (Acts 13:1)

Greet Andronicus and Junia, my relatives (or compatriots) who were in prison with me; they are prominent among the apostles, and they were in Christ before I was. (Rom. 16:7)

Greet Rufus, chosen in the Lord, and greet his mother— a mother to me also. (Rom. 16:13)

I have used these few threads from the New Testament to weave this story about Simon of Cyrene, his two sons, Alexander and Rufus, and Lucius of Cyrene.

I have made several assumptions. I have assumed that Alexander and Rufus, the sons of Simon of Cyrene, became followers of Jesus Christ, and that is why Mark inserted their names in the gospel he wrote. The Christians for whom Mark wrote his gospel may well have known them. I have also assumed the Rufus mentioned by Mark in his gospel is the same Rufus to whom Paul sent greetings in his letter to the church at Rome. I believe these are reasonable assumptions.

There are several inferences, too, that one can draw from the Bible verses on which this story is based. It is reasonable to believe there was a significant Jewish community in Cyrene. We know Simon was a part of that community and was present in Jerusalem to celebrate Passover in the year Jesus was crucified. Further, there were Jews from Cyrene in Jerusalem on the day of Pentecost. Again we may believe that since Cyrene is named as one of the areas from which people came to celebrate that festival, at least some of those people must have become followers of Jesus and been baptized. We may accept that Simon and Lucius knew one another since they were from the same city in the northeast corner of what is Libya today. Perhaps they were members of the same Jewish congregation in that city. They may not have been brothers-in-law, as I have made them in this story, but they probably would have known one another. Finally, there is a tradition that Mark, the author of the second gospel, was from the Pentapolis, five cities including Cyrene located in that area of North Africa.

The characters in this story who are not named in the New Testament are fictional. The crucifixion and resurrection of Jesus, the miracle of Pentecost, the Council in Jerusalem, and the accounts concerning the apostle Paul's conversion and missionary journeys are taken from the New Testament records. The burning of Rome followed by the persecution of Christians, who were accused of setting the fire, is supported by historical records. Other events in this story are fictional.

While most of this story would be labeled a novel, a story that did not happen, I would argue that it could have happened. Whether this story has any relationship to what actually happened is a matter for debate. However, in writing this story, my intent is not to present an accurate historical record of what happened to people from Cyrene in the middle of the first century of this era. The real purpose I have for writing this story is to present information about what happened to the followers of Jesus in Christian congregations during the first few decades after the resurrection of Jesus. I have attempted to be faithful to what we know about the growth and development of the Christian church in those years, and I have tried to remain true to the geography of the area and the historical events in the years from AD 30 to 65.

I have one concern in writing this story: that I do not write anything that could be construed as derogatory toward Judaism. The fact is that the Christian church grew from roots in Judaism, and in the first twenty years after the day of Pentecost in AD 30, the church gradually moved away from its Jewish roots. The decisions affirmed at the Council in Jerusalem made this separation permanent. I have attempted to describe this process accurately and with sensitivity toward our Jewish brothers and sisters. My personal belief is that the Jewish people were and continue to be the chosen people of God, because the promises God makes are irrevocable.

My hope in writing this story is that as you, the reader, make your way through the narrative, your faith and spiritual experience may be enriched and in some way this story will inspire in you a greater commitment to and a deeper understanding of the love of God as it has been revealed to us in Jesus Christ.

There are four people who deserve special commendation and appreciation for the assistance they have given me in this project. My wife, Trudy, has given invaluable advice concerning the plot and the development of the story. She is also an excellent proofreader, and I depend on her skill to proof everything I write. Our friend Kate McCamish read and edited the manuscript and made important suggestions that improved the text. An artist friend, Susan Mather, MD, created the cover picture for the book and my daughter-in- law Marilee Neff took the author's picture. I thank all four of them for the work they have done to enhance and enrich this story. Any defects that may remain are my responsibility alone.

H. Richard Neff

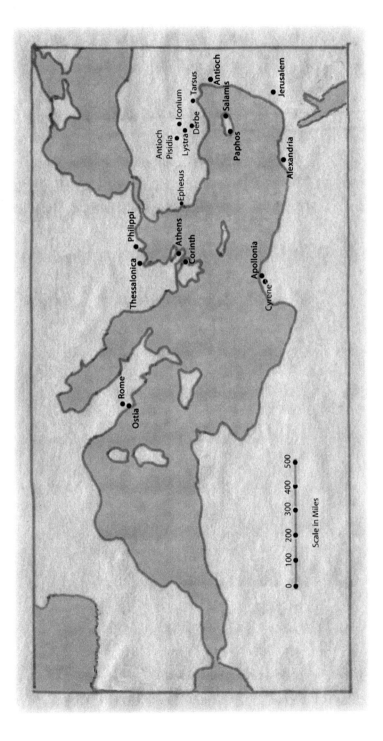

LIST OF SIGNIFICANT CHARACTERS

Simon: Wheat farmer in Cyrene who carries Jesus' cross
Miriam: Simon's wife
Alexander: Simon's older son
Rufus: Simon's younger son
Rabbi Samuel: Rabbi in Cyrene
Lucius: Simon's brother-in-law and a leader in the church in Antioch
Jonathan: Teacher, traveler to Jerusalem, and leader in Cyrene church
Naomi: Jonathan's wife
Suzanna: Jonathan and Naomi's daughter, who becomes Rufus's wife
Isaac: Simon's good friend, farmer and traveler to Jerusalem
Ruth: Isaac's wife
Daniel: Grows figs, traveler to Jerusalem, convert at Pentecost
Judith: Daniel's wife
Seth: Daniel's brother
Rachel: Seth's wife
Joel: Architect and carpenter, traveler to Jerusalem
Hannah: Joel's wife
Levi: Host to group in Jerusalem
Anna: Levi's wife and hostess to group in Jerusalem
Caleb: Simon's brother, also a farmer
Esther: Caleb's wife
Joseph: Lucius and Miriam's older brother

Sarah:	Joseph's wife
Rebekah:	Joseph, Miriam, and Lucius's mother
Joanna:	Miriam's friend
Matthew:	Joanna's husband
Gaius:	Simon and Miriam's Gentile neighbor and blacksmith in Cyrene
Julia:	Gaius's wife
Olivia:	Gaius and Julia's daughter, who becomes Alexander's wife
Naomi:	Rufus and Suzanna's first daughter, born in Cyrene
Mary:	Rufus and Suzanna's second daughter, born in Rome
Mark:	Gospel writer
Andronicus:	Leader of congregation in Rome and apostle
Junia:	Andronicus's wife and apostle
Paul:	Christian apostle and missionary
Barnabas:	Mark's uncle and Christian missionary
Lydia:	Christian leader in Philippi
Peter:	Disciple of Jesus
Aquila:	Christian leader and fellow worker with Paul in Corinth
Priscilla:	Wife of Aquila and Christian leader
Claudius:	Roman emperor (AD 41-54)
Nero:	Roman emperor (AD 54-68)

1

—⁓•◦◖◗◦•⁓—

SIMON

The sun is halfway up in the eastern sky, creating a bright and beautiful Sabbath; no clouds can be seen anywhere. The warmth of the sunlight is lifting the temperature from the morning chill to a very comfortable level.

My family and I are hurrying down the street. We are late for the Sabbath service at our synagogue. To our left, pillars mark one side of the temple of Apollo, a reminder of the glory Cyrene enjoyed several centuries ago when it was a beautiful and prosperous Greek colony. Miriam, my wife, can hardly keep pace with my long strides, and our two boys, Alexander and Rufus, are running to stay close to us. I am tall, standing half a head above the other men in Cyrene, and at thirty-five years, I am in the prime of life. Miriam, ten years my junior, is a very beautiful and capable woman. We have been happily married for just over ten years. Our son, Alexander is a very active eight-year-old, and Rufus, our other boy, is now five. We are very faithful to the laws and traditions of our Jewish faith. That is why I am hurrying to arrive on time at the synagogue for worship on this Sabbath day.

"I don't know why the good Lord made that mare go into labor this morning," I mutter to myself as I rush down the street. "I knew I should not be working on the Sabbath, but I had to make sure all would go well as the mare delivered her foal. Now we will be late for Sabbath worship."

Finally Miriam, almost out of breath, implores me with an edge in her voice, "Simon, *please* slow down. I'm hurrying as fast as I can, and I am hardly keeping up. Alexander is running to keep pace, and little Rufus is racing as fast as he can and is falling behind. We're late now. It won't matter if we are a minute or two later."

Still muttering to myself about the mare and her foal, I do slow my pace.

Six miles ahead of us in the distance, the deep blue waters of the Mediterranean Sea glisten in the sunlight. But I don't have time to notice the beauty of the scenery. I've seen it many times before. We turn a corner onto a side street, rushing past other people who are strolling along the way. Obviously these people are not members of the congregation heading to worship.

Just down the street our synagogue comes into view. It is a square two-story building. The main door is open to the east—toward the holy city, Jerusalem. As we near the open door, we can hear the voices of the worshippers chanting the beautiful words of the entrance song inviting the Lord to be present in our worship.

> Who shall ascend the hill of the Lord? Or who shall stand in his holy place? Those who have clean hands and pure hearts, who do not lift up their souls to what is false, and do not swear deceitfully. They will receive blessing from the Lord, and vindication from the God of their salvation. Such is the company of those who seek him, who seek the face of the God of Jacob. Lift up your heads, O gates! And be lifted up, O ancient doors! that the King of glory may come in. Who is this King of glory? The Lord strong and mighty, The Lord mighty in battle.[1]

Then with voices lifted ever louder in praise, the congregation reaches the climax of the song as the people repeat the chorus:

> Lift up your heads, O gates! And be lifted up, O ancient doors! that the King of glory may come in. Who is this King of glory? The Lord of hosts, He is the King of glory.[2]

As the congregation completes the final words of the song, we slip into place on one of the benches positioned around the *bima,* a small, raised platform in the middle of the room. On the platform are a wooden pulpit and a chair.

After several readings and the chanting of another song, Elias, the leader of the synagogue council, steps up on the bima and begins the prayer: "Hear, O Israel: The Lord our God, the Lord alone."

The people respond:

> You shall love the Lord your God with all your heart and with all your soul and with all your might. And these words that I command you today shall be on your heart.[3]

As the prayer continues, my attention begins to wander. With a sense of pride, I remember that I sat on these same benches with my father and grandfather when I was young. Now I am here worshipping with my sons, hoping and praying they will be faithful children of the covenant.

It is not easy to be a Jew in Cyrene today. Years ago Jews were accepted as equals, but now that has changed. There are subtle but very real pressures—economic and social—that discriminate against the Jews in Cyrene today. Sometimes these pressures are not too subtle, like the day last week when a gang of ruffians shouted, "Jew, Jew!" at Jacob's son as they chased him down the street and then stood laughing as he ran in fear.

I pray, "Lord, I ask that my sons will not give in to the growing pressure to abandon the traditions of our faith and the faithful worship of you, our Lord and God."

Soon the prayer ends, and Elias, greatly revered by the congregation, sits down on the chair on the bima. One of the attendants hands him a scroll containing the Torah. He opens it to the last book and begins to read about the blessings God will give to those faithful people who are obedient and follow the Law. I latch onto one of the promises in the Torah:

> The Lord will open for you his rich storehouse, the heavens, to give the rain of your land in its season, and to bless all your undertakings.[4]

My winter planting of wheat is growing in the fertile soil of my fields, but Cyrene has not received the normal amount of rain this month. I pray that the rain will come so the wheat will be ready for reaping before the hot, dry weather of the summer months arrives.

The attendant takes the scroll from the Elias's hands, covers it with the blue mantle of the Law, and replaces it in the holy ark. Then he lifts a second scroll from the ark and takes it to another man who has come forward to sit in the chair on the bima. The man begins to read from the prophets. At the conclusion of the reading, the attendant returns the scroll to the holy ark. Rabbi Samuel then takes his place on the bima to teach the lessons he has prepared from the Scripture. I listen intently.

At the end of his instruction, Rabbi Samuel makes a special announcement. He is planning to go to Jerusalem to celebrate Passover this year, and he invites men from the congregation to accompany him on this pilgrimage.

My interest in this journey to Jerusalem is obvious from the attention I pay to this announcement. Miriam, I am certain, will not want me to go, but the dream of traveling to Jerusalem with our rabbi to celebrate Passover is something I am determined I will not miss.

2

———∿∽꩜ᘛꙮᘚ꩜∾∿———

MIRIAM

After our meal, Alexander leaves to find a friend, and Rufus goes to his room to play. Simon and I are alone. A strained silence settles over us. Both of us know we have something very important to discuss, but neither of us wants to begin the conversation. I can tell Simon senses I am not in favor of his going to Jerusalem, and both of us are afraid a real disagreement may occur. Neither one of us wants that to happen.

Finally Simon shifts uncomfortably in his chair and breaks the silence. "I should go out to the stable to check on that mare and her foal."

Before he can rise to go, I touch his arm and interrupt him. "Simon, please stay; we must talk, even though we disagree. I know you want to go to Jerusalem to celebrate Passover with Rabbi Samuel and the other men in our congregation. I saw it in your face the moment our rabbi announced he wanted to take a group of men to Jerusalem to celebrate the holiest of all days in our faith. When you gathered around Rabbi Samuel with all the other men who were questioning him about the journey, I realized you hope to join them on their pilgrimage.

"I understand that you really want to go. I suppose you didn't say definitely you would go—or at least I hope you wouldn't do that without consulting me. You know I don't want you to go. I'm afraid of what might happen to you. There are so many dangers involved in traveling on the sea. Besides, there is too much work for you to do here during that time."

"We can harvest the wheat when I get back," explains Simon. "And if it is ready for reaping before I return, my brother, Caleb, and his crew will begin the job. I am certain everything will work out well while I am gone. Caleb will handle all the necessary work on the farm. You won't have to work in the fields or do anything more than you are doing now."

"I know that, Simon. It's really not the farm work that concerns me. It's the responsibilities you have for me and the boys. You know why I am afraid."

"Around fifteen or twenty men gathered around rabbi after the service. Many of them said they are considering going with him to Jerusalem. Your brother, Lucius, was there. He said he would definitely go. I didn't commit myself to travel with them, but you are right, I do want to go. I'm sure we can work things out here so everything will go on smoothly while I am gone."

My voice grows more insistent. "Lucius has no responsibilities. He isn't married; he has no children. You have responsibilities, Simon. Besides, he was very young when our father died. I don't think he remembers the hardship Father's death caused for Mother, Joseph, and me. All the responsibility fell on us to work and hold the family together. If something should happen to you, Alexander and Rufus are too young to help me the way Joseph and I did when we had to help our mother."

Tears begin to form in my eyes. One brims over and rolls down my cheek. Simon knows why I am so anxious and concerned. He reaches across the table to take my hand in his. I realize he is sorry to cause me such pain. He pauses and looks down before he speaks again.

"I know you are afraid because of what happened to your father, but it was a freak storm that caused the ship he was on to capsize and sink. Those severe storms normally occur only in the winter months. Every now and then one will come in the spring, as happened in your father's case, but that is a very rare event indeed. And your father was crossing from here to Rome with that shipment of horses he was delivering to the military there. The ship was in the open sea. We will be sailing along the coast as we go to Alexandria, and then if we can get another ship in Alexandria, we will hug the coast all the way to Joppa. Nothing will happen to harm us. God will keep us safe."

"That's what my father said, too. But God didn't."

"Hush, my dear, don't say anything blasphemous about God. He will take care of us; you will see."

At this point, a small voice interrupts us. Rufus comes around the corner from his room. "Where are you going, Daddy? May I go with you?"

"No, Rufus, you can't go. Someday you will go to Jerusalem to celebrate Passover in the holy city. Every Jewish man should do that at least one time in his life. I plan to go this year. Your Uncle Lucius is going, too. Can you stay here with Alexander and help take care of things for your mother?"

"Sure I can," affirms Rufus. "Alexander and I will take good care of everything while you are away."

My son's words bring a smile to my face even as I brush away the tears that continue to roll down my cheeks.

"I'm going to the stable to check on the new colt," says Simon. "Do you want to go with me, Rufus?"

"Yes, yes. Let's go."

3

RABBI SAMUEL

D awn is breaking. In the first light of day, I open the doors of the synagogue and step out from the darkness within. The twelve men who are accompanying me to Jerusalem are at the bottom of the steps. Each man has a small roll of his possessions at his feet. The men quickly turn from their conversation to face me.

I immediately greet them with a strong, *"Shalom!"* and thank them for deciding to accompany me on this pilgrimage to Jerusalem. Then I recite a psalm.

> I was glad when they said to me, "Let us go to the house of the Lord." Our feet have been standing within your gates, O Jerusalem! Jerusalem is built as a city that is bound firmly together. To it the tribes go up, the tribes of the Lord, as was decreed for Israel, to give thanks to the name of the Lord.[5]

After the psalm I offer a prayer, a blessing for these men and for our travels together. Finally we all recite a psalm that reassures us we will have safe travels.

> I lift up my eyes to the hills—from where will my help come? My help comes from the Lord, who made heaven and earth. He will not let your foot be moved; He who keeps you

will not slumber. He who keeps Israel will neither slumber nor sleep. The Lord is your keeper; the Lord is your shade at your right hand. The sun shall not strike you by day, nor the moon by night. The Lord will keep you from all evil; He will keep your life. The Lord will keep your going out and your coming in from this time on and forevermore. [6]

I overhear Simon saying quietly to Lucius, "I wish Miriam were here. The promise in those words might convince her we will return home safely. She is so worried that something terrible will happen; I understand her fear, but I am sure the Lord will give us safe travels."

Simon spoke to me about Miriam's anxiety and I certainly can understand her fear. I was here in Cyrene when her father died in that terrible storm at sea. The whole family was devastated and it was difficult for them to carry on the successful business Miriam's father had created. I am happy Miriam was persuaded that Simon could accompany me on this journey. He is certainly a fine person.

Now we are ready to depart. I pick up my roll of possessions and begin to walk down the streets of Cyrene toward the coastal town of Apollonia, where we will board the ship for the first leg of our journey, the voyage to Alexandria. The men take one last look at the hills behind the synagogue, where their homes are. Then they pick up their belongings and fall in behind me. A few people look out from their doorways as we pass, but most people in Cyrene are only beginning to awaken for their work this day.

I am really happy with the response I received from my announcement about this pilgrimage. All these men are faithful members of the congregation. Lucius is the youngest of the group. He raises horses with his brother, Joseph, on the farm that was left to them when their father died. Simon, of course, is a farmer. His main crop is wheat, some of which he exports to cities around the Mediterranean, and some he mills into flour to sell at the local market. Like all the farmers in the area, he also has a few olive trees in a grove to produce the fruit from which he presses olive oil and some grape vines to supply wine, mainly for his family's use. Jacob is the one who has extensive vineyards, and the wine he makes each year supplies most of the needs of the synagogue and families in our congregation.

Isaac is a farmer, too. He is Simon's closest friend. He grows both barley and wheat. Some of his grain is being loaded on the ship that will take us to Alexandria. Eli has a large olive grove, and the olive oil he produces is an important commodity in the Pentapolis that includes Cyrene with its port city of Apollonia and the nearby cities of Taucheira, Euesperides, Balagrae, and Barce.

The rich soil in the region where Cyrene is located makes it a center for agriculture. Silphium, an herb that was considered a medicinal cure and an aphrodisiac, was grown only in the area around Cyrene when it was a prosperous Greek colony. That is what made Cyrene an important center for commerce six hundred years ago. Although the demand for silphium has died, Daniel, who is walking with the others toward Apollonia, still grows a little of it. His main crop, however, is figs. His grove of fig trees is among the largest in the area.

Amos raises sheep and goats. He is a very successful man. He spins the wool he shears and sells the yarn to people in the Pentapolis, who then weave their families' clothing and blankets on standing looms in their homes. Amos also milks his herd of goats and sells the milk in the local market. Joel is an architect and carpenter who has business in all five cities of the Pentapolis. He is perhaps the most prosperous man in the group. Noah is an artisan who creates beautiful pieces of silver jewelry that he sells from a shop next to his home.

Nathan, Enos, and Jonathan round out the group. They are teachers in the academies that are a part of the educational system in Cyrene. The city was an important center for education when it was a Greek colony. In those days, it had a medical school and a number of academies. The medical school and some of the academies closed many years ago, but some of the academies continue to educate children and young people today. Nathan, Enos, and Jonathan are all very intelligent men who are well respected for their work. Nathan teaches mathematics. Enos teaches poetry and language arts, and he assists me by teaching Hebrew in the synagogue school. Jonathan is a scientist and astronomer who has the reputation of being one of the best teachers in all the five cities of the Pentapolis.

I am indeed very proud of these men and glad they have decided to go on this Passover pilgrimage. Certainly their faith will be enriched by celebrating Passover in our Holy City.

As the sun is coming up, we enter Apollonia and quickly head for the pier to board the ship that will take us to Alexandria. As we approach the ship, the dock hands are still loading the bags of wheat the ship will carry on this leg of our voyage. We form a line to walk up the gangway. The captain greets us and shows us where we should stow our possessions. Then he returns to the task of supervising the men loading the last few bags of wheat.

A gentle breeze is blowing. When all the wheat is on board, the dock hands pull back the gangplank and untie the lines securing the ship. The sails are unfurled, and the breeze out of the west begins to push our ship eastward along the African coast. Our voyage to Jerusalem has begun.

We passengers stand along the rail on the starboard side of the ship. There is excited conversation about the journey ahead. We watch as Apollonia and Cyrene grow smaller and smaller in the distance until they finally slip from view below the horizon.

We are on our way to Jerusalem!

4

~∞∽ᴏᴄᴦᴏ᷑ᴏᴦᴇᴐᴏᴍ~

SIMON

The voyage from Cyrene to Alexandria takes just five days. We are ahead of schedule. The winds from the northwest and the calm seas have made this leg of our journey very pleasant indeed. We have had plenty of opportunity on board the ship to talk and get to know one another in ways we never could have back in Cyrene.

When the famous lighthouse of Alexandria appears on the horizon, we rush to the bow to view this magnificent structure. After our ship docks in Alexandria, we disembark. Immediately we begin making inquiries to locate another ship traveling on to Joppa. No captain has a trip scheduled for that leg of our journey, so we contact leaders in the Jewish community in Alexandria and join a group traveling to Jerusalem on camels and donkeys.

We arrive in Jerusalem a full week before Passover. The first sight of the holy city takes our breath away. Praise God for our good fortune in being here, and thank God for our safe journey! What a beautiful sight it is to walk toward holy Jerusalem! We enter the city by the southern gate, and from there we see the temple ahead and on our right. That is our destination.

We want to go there as quickly as possible, but we are not ritually clean; in fact, we are not clean at all. We are covered with dust and grime from our journey, so we immediately hurry to the home where we will stay. Joel's brother and sister-in-law, Levi and Anna, have a large home just inside the west wall in the area known as the Upper City. They welcome us warmly and show us the rooms where we will stay. Anna, who is the consummate hostess, repeats several times as she shows us our rooms, "I'm so sorry we have to crowd three or four of you in each room. I wish we had a larger home so you would be more comfortable during your visit."

We respond over and over, "The space you have for us is quite adequate. We are so grateful to you and Levi for inviting us to be your guests while we are here in Jerusalem. It is a thrill for us to be here and we look forward to celebrating Passover in your home."

Thirteen extra men crowded into the home create some problems for our host and hostess. Their two sons have to move their possessions into some storage space to make room for us. We know, however, that we are very fortunate. At Passover time pilgrims from every part of the Mediterranean world take up all available space in homes in the city as well as in the villages of Bethany, Bethpage, and other nearby towns; some even as far away as Emmaus. Those who do not find space in a home or inn put up tents outside the city walls and sleep in them until they are ready to return home. Thousands of people will soon occupy every available niche in and around the city.

We put our things in the different rooms where we will spend the next eight or ten nights. Then we bathe in turn. We are hot and dirty from our travels, but it is more important that we cleanse ourselves ritually before we enter the temple grounds.

Having bathed and put on fresh clothing, we hurry to the temple. We enter the temple grounds through one of the two gates in the west wall leading in from the Upper City. Magnificent columns support the porticos all around the temple. We walk along the Royal Portico and then pass through a gate in the south wall to enter the Court of the Gentiles. Inside the Court of the Gentiles, there are some booths along one wall where men are selling animals and birds for sacrifice. We pass these booths and go around to the east side of the wall separating the Court of the Gentiles from the Court of the Women.

We climb the fourteen steps that lead up to the Beautiful Gate and pass through to enter the Court of the Women. This is the area in the temple grounds where Jewish women come to worship. We hurry across the Court of the Women. Ahead of us is Nicanor's Gate, which gives us access to the Court of Israel. The gate itself is huge, and when we pass through it, we have a full view of the temple, our holiest building.

The temple rises before us in all its glorious splendor. The temple is about 150 feet long and at its highest point reaches 180 feet. I have never seen such a large building. We have nothing like it in Cyrene. Even the temple of Apollo there is not so grand. We all stand in awe. Four huge pillars in the front of the temple support the roof over the porch, which is also known as the vestibule.

A small wall about a foot and a half high serves as a partition between the inner area of the court restricted for the priests and the outer area where Jewish men assemble to worship. The altar of burnt offering is in the priestly area in front of the temple. The altar is seventy-five feet square and some twenty feet high. There is a ramp the priests use to approach it.

Twelve steps lead up to the vestibule of the temple. The vestibule is decorated with gold and has a large gold vine with a huge cluster of golden grapes hanging from it. The thrill of being in this place is overwhelming; all we can do is quietly walk around to take in the wonder of the temple. In the next few days, we will gather again and again in the Court of Israel to worship.

5

———∿∿⊙⊙⊙⊙∿∿———

LUCIUS

W e had been in Jerusalem for only a few days when Jonathan and I, returning from a walk outside the city wall, report to Levi and our friends from Cyrene about a very curious sight we observed when we approached the gate into the city.

Jonathan describes the scene: "We were coming down the road from the north on our way to the city gate when a procession approached. Naturally we stepped off to the side of the road to watch. There was a man riding a donkey. The people with him were repeating over and over again, 'Hosanna, blessed is he who comes in the name of the Lord.' They were waving palm branches as they shouted their hosannas."

"I understand the symbolism of this demonstration," I continue. "We all know what our Prophet Zechariah wrote: 'Rejoice greatly, O daughter of Zion! Shout aloud, O daughter of Jerusalem! Lo, your king comes to you; triumphant and victorious is he, humble and riding on a donkey, on a colt, the foal of a donkey.'[7] Could this possibly be the Messiah? Someone said his name is Jesus."

"I've heard of him," says Levi. "He is an itinerant preacher from Nazareth, a village that is a three-day journey north of here in Galilee. He began teaching and preaching about three years ago. He has quite a following in Galilee, his home province. There are some people in Jerusalem, and in Bethany and Bethpage, who are followers and friends of his too. There are even a few families here in Jerusalem who've heard

15

him preach. They say he is a very charismatic leader. What troubles me, however, is that he has entered the city in this way."

"Why be concerned?" asks Jonathan.

"Well, any time the city is so full of people for one of our holy days, the Roman officials bring in reinforcements to make sure there are no disturbances. The priests and temple officials, too, will act quickly to quell any kind of demonstration because they don't want the Romans to think they cannot keep peace among our people. If Jesus, or anyone else for that matter, were to create a disturbance, the officials will send armed soldiers to crush any demonstration that could possibly get out of hand. That procession you saw could create problems if it appears that Jesus' followers are trying to advance the claim that he really is the Messiah, who will come to overturn the rule of Rome. Let's hope they don't make trouble this year."

"Has there been trouble other years?" asks Jonathan.

"Oh, yes. Several years ago there was a man who claimed to be the Messiah. He brought his band of rebels into the city and began to battle a small group of Roman soldiers. Soon reinforcements arrived, and the soldiers killed most of the people among his rebel band. The few who survived the engagement were captured, taken outside the city walls, and crucified."

Then Daniel and Amos come through the door. They are returning from the temple.

"Levi, who is this person named Jesus?" asks Daniel. "When Amos and I were coming through the Court of the Gentiles on our way back to your home, a man and his followers began to overturn the tables of the people in those booths along the wall where they sell birds and animals for sacrifice. We watched in amazement. Who would dare do something like that! Some people said that the man's name is Jesus. Do you know anything about him?"

"Oh no!" Levi exclaims. "That's terrible news. The temple officials will never let him get away with that. This Jesus is now a marked man. The temple police and the Roman soldiers will watch his every move. If he or any of his followers do anything that suggests they may make some move to begin a revolution, they will be arrested and dealt with immediately. I'm glad my feet are not in their sandals."

6

---〜ᗐᘉ᠔ᙍᗢᙍᘉ᠔〜---

RABBI SAMUEL

Dawn is breaking as we prepare for our Passover celebration. At sundown we will have our Passover meal. The blare of trumpets blown from the highest point of the temple resounds over the city. This is the signal for all the Jewish men in the city to bring a lamb between eight days and one year old to the temple to be killed and prepared ritually for the Passover meal.

We purchased our lamb yesterday. Our group is scheduled to come to the temple in the third hour to prepare the lamb for our Passover celebration. There are sixteen of us—the twelve who came with me from Cyrene, Levi, his two sons, and me.

At the appointed hour, we approach the temple carrying our Passover lamb. We enter the temple grounds and pass through the Court of the Gentiles and the Court of the Women until we stand before the temple itself.

Many other men are gathered and waiting at that low wall separating the area for the priest from the congregation. Slowly we make our way through the crowd. When it is our turn, we hand our lamb to one of the priests.

We watch while the priest slits the throat of the lamb with his knife. The bleating of the lamb grows weaker as the life drains from it. Another priest has caught the blood of the lamb in a silver bowl. He takes that up the incline to the altar and dashes the lamb's blood against the foot

17

of the altar. Our lamb is handed back to us, and we hang the carcass on a peg in the wall separating the Court of Israel from the Court of the Women. There we flay and dress our Passover lamb. Levi takes the fat of the lamb to one of the priests, who offers it on the altar.

While all of this takes place, a chorus of Levites chants from the psalms.

> I love the Lord, because he has heard my voice and my supplications. Because he inclined his ear to me; therefore I will call on him as long as I live. The snares of death encompassed me, the pangs of Sheol laid hold on me, I suffered distress and anguish. Then I called on the name of the Lord: "O Lord, I pray, save my life!" Gracious is the Lord, and righteous; our God is merciful.[8]

When the ritual preparation of the lamb is complete, we return to Levi's home. There we skewer the lamb on a spit made of pomegranate wood and begin to roast it over an open fire. Meanwhile Anna prepares all of the other food for our Passover meal.

On the previous day, Levi and Anna had removed all the leavened bread from their home and thoroughly cleaned each room. Anna put away the ordinary utensils used in the kitchen and replaced them with those that are reserved for use at Passover. Now she is preparing the *matzah*, the bitter herbs, and the *haroseth* for the Seder. By late afternoon, everything is ready for our Passover ritual to begin.

Just after sunset we gather around the table dressed in our finest clothing. There are four empty cups at each place. Levi fills one cup for each of us with red wine while I pronounce the blessing. Then Levi pours water from a pitcher for the ritual cleansing of our hands as we recline on our left sides at the table.

I begin, "We praise God, Ruler of everything, who has kept us alive, raised us up, and brought us to this happy moment." Then we drink the first cup of wine.

We dip a sprig of a green vegetable in salt water to remind us of the tears our ancestors shed when they were slaves. Then I take the middle of the three pieces of matzah that are on the table and break it to remind us of the hurried flight of our ancestors from Egypt. Levi then pours red wine into the second cup at each place.

At this point Aaron, Levi and Anna's younger son, opens the ritual of the Passover questions by asking his father the central question that begins the telling of the story of the Exodus from Egypt: "Why is this night different from all other nights?"

Levi responds by reciting a brief review of our history that is in the Torah:

> "A wandering Aramean was my ancestor; he went down into Egypt and lived there as an alien, few in number, and there he became a great nation, mighty and populous. When the Egyptians treated us harshly and afflicted us, by imposing hard labor on us, we cried to the Lord, the God of our ancestors; the Lord heard our voice and saw our affliction, our toil, and our oppression. The Lord brought us out of Egypt with a mighty hand and an outstretched arm, with a terrifying display of power, and with signs and wonders; and he brought us into this place and gave us this land, a land flowing with milk and honey.[9]

Aaron then continues this ritual by asking the four questions that explain the meaning of the Passover meal.

"Why is it that on all other nights during the year we eat either bread or matzah, but on this night we eat only matzah?"

Levi responds, "We eat only matzah because our ancestors could not wait for the bread to rise when they were fleeing slavery in Egypt, so they took the bread out of their ovens while it was still flat; that is matzah."

Then Aaron asks his next question. "Why is it that on all other nights we eat all kinds of vegetables, but on this night we eat only bitter herbs?"

Levi answers, "We eat only *maror*, a bitter herb, to remind us of the bitterness of slavery our ancestors endured in Egypt."

"Why is it that on all other nights we do not dip our herbs even once, but on this night we dip them twice?" asks Aaron.

"We dip twice, first green vegetables in salt water symbolizing the replacing of tears with gratefulness, and a second time dipping maror in charoset, a sweet mixture of nuts and wine, to symbolize the sweetening of the burden of bitterness and suffering to lessen its pain," explains Levi.

Finally Aaron asks, "On all other nights we eat meat that has been roasted, stewed, or boiled; why on this night do we eat only roasted meat?"

Levi answers, "When our ancestors prepared to leave slavery in Egypt, the Lord told them to kill a lamb, splash its blood on the doorposts and lintel of the house, and then roast the lamb and eat all of it."

Then I elaborate on the story Levi told from our scriptures: "Our ancestor, Abraham, left his home in Ur to go out to a place God would show him. In faith he went as he had been instructed. God led him to this land and promised to make his descendants so numerous they could not be counted. In time the descendants of Abraham went into Egypt to escape a famine. After a long sojourn in Egypt they were enslaved. Then God raised up Moses to lead the people out of slavery in Egypt and bring them to the Promised Land. God inflicted ten plagues upon the Egyptians before they would permit our people to leave. The last plague, the death of the firstborn in each family, was the occasion of our Passover; the Angel of Death passed over our homes and only visited the homes of the Egyptians. Pharaoh permitted our people to go, which they did. Then Pharaoh changed his mind and sent his army to pursue us. God parted the waters of the sea to allow our people to escape the pursuing Egyptian army. Our ancestors wandered in the wilderness for forty years before they came into the land God had promised to them. If God had not performed the miracles that gave us our freedom, we would still be slaves in Egypt."

At that point in our Passover ritual, we drink the second cup of wine.

The ritual washing of our hands takes place again, and I pronounce the customary blessing before eating bread. We take a small piece of matzah to eat it. We dip the bitter herbs that symbolize the hardships of the journey from Egypt in the charoset and place it between two small pieces of matzah. Then we eat it.

Anna serves the Seder meal, and we all eat. After the meal, we eat a half-matzah. Then Levi fills the third cup at each place with wine, and after I pronounce the blessing over the wine, we drink.

At the end of the meal, Levi pours red wine into the cup of Elijah and the fourth cup of all who are at the table, and we recite the passage in which we invite the prophet Elijah to come heralding the arrival of the Messiah.

> Elijah the prophet, the returning, the man of Gilead: return to us speedily, in our days with the Messiah, the son of David.

Finally we offer a psalm of praise to God and we drink the fourth cup of wine. We have celebrated the liberation of our people from slavery in Egypt, and we have done it in our holy city, Jerusalem. Praise be to God!

7

———∞∙∘⊙⊙⊙∘∙∞———

SIMON

At daybreak the morning after our Passover meal, Lucius and I leave our lodging to explore the countryside beyond the city walls. We walk several miles, taking in the scenes of the farms and pasture land. We talk about how these areas are so different from our farm land in Cyrene.

"We are so fortunate at home to have fields with such deep and rich topsoil where we can plant our crops. I wouldn't want to try to grow wheat in these fields. The soil is so shallow and rocky."

"Yes," replies Lucius, "and obviously they do not get enough rain here to provide the lush pasture we have at home. They must have to move their flocks of sheep to new pasture almost every day."

We walk in silence for several minutes. Our conversation about the land around Cyrene directs our thoughts to family and home.

"I feel bad that my coming on this pilgrimage created such fear for Miriam. I did not want to miss the opportunity to see the temple and to celebrate Passover in our holy city. But I do deeply regret causing Miriam to have such anxiety over my coming here. I'm not sure she will ever board a ship to travel anywhere and I doubt that she will ever consent to our boys sailing anywhere."

"I was so young when Father died," Lucius said. "I have only vague memories of those days. I can still see our mother trying to hide her tears from me. And I remember Joseph, young as he was, working day and night to continue Father's business. He had learned from our father how to breed and care for the horses and he had pestered Father to allow him to travel with him that spring to deliver the horses to the soldiers in Rome. It really would have been a double tragedy for our family if Father had permitted him to go.

"I don't remember much about Miriam's reaction to our father's death, but obviously that tragedy had a lasting effect on her. In her mind the sea is a very fearsome place."

Engrossed in our conversation we walk a little farther than we had planned. The sun is moving up in the eastern sky when we decide we had better retrace out steps and return to Jerusalem.

As we come along a road that is crowded with other pilgrims, we notice a centurion on horseback approaching us. Because of the many people on the road, we do not immediately see who is following him or what they are doing. As the people in front of us step to the side of the road, a group of Roman soldiers behind the centurion comes into view. Of course, Lucius and I step off the road also to let the soldiers pass.

Then we notice for the first time that the soldiers are forcing three men with roughhewn crossbars on their shoulders to walk along behind the centurion's horse. Every time their prisoners slow a bit, the soldiers lash them with whips. One of the prisoners obviously has been scourged; the back of his cloak is covered with blood. Drops of blood trickle down his brow from the puncture wounds caused by a ring of thorns cruelly pressed down on his head. As I take in the horror of this scene, I am filled with pity for the one who has been beaten so severely.

I cannot take my eyes off this man as he approaches. He does not have the appearance of a criminal deserving such harsh punishment. Even though the pain he is experiencing must be excruciating, his eyes have a kind expression. As he comes toward Lucius and me, he stumbles and goes down on one knee. A soldier lashes him and forces him to his feet. I flinch, bite my lip, and turn my head away as the whip comes down on the raw wounds on his back. How brutal is that soldier!

The prisoner rises under the cruel weight of the crossbar, takes a few more steps, and then stumbles and falls again, this time on both hands and knees. The heavy crossbar falls from his shoulder, and with a thud, it hits the ground. After a few more blows with his whip, the soldier finally realizes his prisoner can no longer carry his burden.

The soldier scans the crowd. He fixes his gaze on me. "You there, carry this man's cross up the road to the place where we will crucify these criminals."

I look around, hoping the soldier is pointing to a person beside or behind me. "No, you," he commands. "You look like you're strong enough."

"Who? Who me?" I stammer, hoping I can escape this onerous task.

"Yes, you," orders the soldier, "get out here and pick up that cross."

I step out and shoulder the man's burden. Despite his weakness and his pain, he looks at me with an expression of sincere kindness and gratitude. That kind gaze strikes deep in my heart. I cannot believe that any man suffering such intense pain could look at another with such love and gratitude. I fall in step with the soldiers as we walk to the place of crucifixion. Lucius follows us. When we come to the place where these three are to be crucified, I am relieved of my burden. The crosses are by the side of the road in full view of everyone so all who pass may be reminded of what will happen to one who causes trouble.

The soldiers hammer six-inch-long iron nails into the condemned men's wrists, pinning them to the crossbar. Then they lift the crossbars onto the vertical beam already in place. The remaining nails they drive through the prisoners' feet into the vertical pole on which the crossbars are attached. Blood begins to ooze from their wounds as they hang there to die. I cannot take my eyes off the man whose cross I carried. He obviously is suffering great pain, but there is something compelling about him that grips my attention. His eyes, his face, his whole bearing belie the suffering he obviously is experiencing. He seems resigned to his fate but still appears to be confident, trusting in God.

I join Lucius on the other side of the road. He is standing with some people who followed this gruesome procession. Most of them are women who are weeping and lamenting the terrible fate of their friend. The women stand by the side of the road, crying and hugging to console one another.

I have never seen anyone being crucified before. It is a terrible sight.

Lucius whispers to me, "They say his name is Jesus. The Sanhedrin convicted him of blasphemy early this morning."

I remember what Levi had said about this Jesus of Nazareth. Indeed he is a marked man, another would-be Messiah yearning to set our people free.

We stay there for a while; I'm not sure how long. But after some time has passed, Jesus' head bows, with his chin resting on his chest. His eyes close, and his lips move. He seems to be speaking, but I cannot make out the words. His suffering obviously is intense as he gasps for breath and his life slowly and painfully ebbs away. I can no longer bear the sight of his dying. May God be merciful to him!

Lucius and I leave the crucifixion scene to go back to Jerusalem. We walk slowly and in silence, the terrible crucifixion scene indelibly imprinted in our minds.

It is almost noon when Lucius and I arrive at Levi's house. Everyone notices how troubled we are. Slowly, painfully, I tell the story of our experience. Lucius fills in some details, mainly the information he received from the women who gathered at the foot of Jesus' cross.

Rabbi Samuel cuts off the conversation by blurting out, "If he is guilty of blasphemy, he deserves to die."

I cannot believe such a cruel statement is coming from our rabbi. The compassionate man I saw could not be a blasphemer or a heretic, and certainly he did not deserve to die so cruel a death. But I keep my thoughts to myself.

About the time Rabbi Samuel utters his hateful remark, dark clouds seal off the light of the sun. It is almost as dark as night, and it stays that way until mid-afternoon. Then the ground under our feet trembles. The world seems to be coming apart.

That evening we eat in silence, and at sundown, the beginning of the Sabbath, Anna lights the candles and Rabbi Samuel leads our worship. After that I am ready to be by myself. I retire to the room I am sharing with Isaac and Eli and try to sleep. But I cannot. The terrible image of the crucifixion of Jesus keeps appearing in my mind as I toss and turn. When Isaac and Eli come into the room to retire for the night,

I try to be quiet, pretending I am already asleep. Even after they are asleep, I cannot get any rest. The injustice of it all! The horrible beating! The bloody back! The cruel nails! And that crown of thorns! What a travesty of justice it was! Blasphemy, nonsense! It was simply the cruelest form of punishment, and it was completely undeserved.

Finally, in the middle of the night I can lie there no longer. Quietly I arise, put on my robe and sandals, and leave the house. I walk down the street and through the gate in the city wall to hurry to the site of the crucifixion.

As I approach, I can see in the darkness that the cross on which Jesus hung is empty. The centurion sees me approaching and advances toward me from the cluster of soldiers gathered around a small fire behind the crosses. The other two men are still hanging there. They will soon die.

The centurion challenges me. "What are you doing here at this time of night?"

"I came to see what happened to Jesus. I—I was the one who carried his cross, you remember," I stammer.

"I don't remember, but he died before sundown. Some of his friends lowered his body from the cross and took it to a tomb that some wealthy man offered to them."

"He did not deserve to die," I volunteer.

"You're right; he was an innocent man," says the centurion.

"Then why did you crucify him?" I ask.

"We are under orders. We do what we are told to do." With a wave of his hand, he dismisses me.

I turn slowly to retrace my steps into the city. With head bowed and filled with deep sorrow, I trudge back to the city and to Levi and Anna's home. The joy of Passover, the celebration of freedom for our people, is completely ruined for me by the horrible memory of this crucifixion. I am ready to leave Jerusalem to return to Cyrene and the familiar surroundings at home. But I will never be able to erase from my memory the terrible scenes I have witnessed today.

8

ALEXANDER

When our father returns from Jerusalem, Rufus and I are surprised by the change in his mood. We thought he would be excited and happy about all the new places he had visited and everything he had seen during his journey. We expected him to tell us all about his experiences. Surely he would be overjoyed at celebrating Passover in our holy city. But he hardly speaks to us about his trip. He is moody and troubled. Mother says he is depressed, whatever that is.

The wheat crop was ready to be harvested when Father returned, so he and the men who work on our farm are busy from morning until evening cutting the stalks of wheat, binding them in sheaves, and then eventually bringing the sheaves to the threshing floor, where they separate the wheat from the chaff.

I am too young to help, but I watch everything the workers do. Someday I will work with them. I guess it's good that Father is so busy. His work takes his mind off whatever is bothering him.

One evening I overhear a conversation Father is having with Mother. I hear Father say, "I was singled out from a crowd of people to carry the cross for a man who was being taken out of the city to be crucified. It was a terrible experience to see a man, who even the centurion said was innocent of any crime, being nailed to a cross and left there to die."

"How terrible!" Mother says, "why would they crucify an innocent man?"

"They said he was guilty of blasphemy," explains Father.

"Well blasphemy is a sin, but it is hardly a reason to condemn a person to die."

I don't really understand what they are talking about. I don't know what blasphemy is and to nail a person to a cross sounds like a cruel thing to do.

Several weeks later Father begins to tell Rufus and me some things about his trip. He describes the temple in Jerusalem. "The temple grounds cover a very large area. There is an outer wall with a roof supported by stone columns. When you enter through one of the gates you are in the Court of the Gentiles. Anyone can go into that area of the temple grounds. There is another wall that separates the Court of the Gentiles from the next area. You climb some steps and go through a gate called the Beautiful Gate and you are in the Court of the Women where Jewish women go to pray. Another wall is inside the Court of the Women and when you go through a gate in that wall you enter the Court of Israel where Jewish men go to worship. There you have a full view of our temple, a magnificent building larger than anything we have here in Cyrene."

"Even larger than the temple of Apollo here in Cyrene?" I ask.

"Oh, yes, even larger than that building, and much more beautiful."

I am amazed that any building could be as large as the temple to a Greek god here in Cyrene.

"Father, I heard you talking to Mother several weeks ago about a man you had to help carry a cross." I could tell immediately from the look that came over Father's face that he wished I had not brought up that subject, but I continued anyway. "You said this man was guilty of blasphemy and that he was crucified. What is blasphemy and what does it mean to be crucified?"

"Well, blasphemy is saying anything that is disrespectful or false about our God, and crucifixion is the way Roman soldiers kill criminals. I understand this man, Jesus was his name, said that he was the Messiah God sent to free our people from Roman rule. The priests said that was claiming to be like God, obviously a false claim concerning his relationship with God. That's why they crucified him. He was so weak from being beaten that he stumbled and fell right where I was standing. A Roman soldier pulled me from a crowd and forced me to carry this man's cross.

I want to learn more so I ask another question. "Father, tell me, what is a messiah?"

Father explains, "The prophets have told us that God will send a person who will deliver our people from oppression. This deliverer is called the Messiah; what that means is that he will come as the anointed one, like a king or emperor, who will set us free and establish again the kingdom of David, our greatest king. He will rule over the entire world and will take away all that is evil and unjust. Because of his rule, everyone in the world will do what is right. There will be peace and righteousness and justice because under his rule everyone will obey the Torah, God's Law."

"Well," I ask, "if this man you saw was such a kind and wonderful person, why could he not be the Messiah?"

"The Messiah," responds Father, "would never die on a cross. Only people who are cursed die on a cross. Our Messiah will be triumphant. His power will be greater than the power of Rome. No, Jesus was not the Messiah. He was a good man. People said he was respected as a preacher and teacher, a rabbi. He healed people who were sick. But he did not defeat Rome and establish a peaceable kingdom in which there is justice and righteousness for all people. No, Jesus is not the Messiah. We are still waiting for the one who will deliver us."

That explanation satisfies me, but only for a time. Uncle Lucius didn't come back to Cyrene with the group that traveled to Jerusalem with Rabbi Samuel. He, Jonathan, and Daniel decided to stay in Jerusalem until the festival of Pentecost. They apparently wanted to make the most of their trip to the holy city. When Uncle Lucius, Jonathan, and Daniel do return from Jerusalem, they have a different story to tell.

9

—⁓⁓∘᥆ℰᵏ∘Ꮹᵏℰ∘᥆⁓⁓—

RUFUS

The hot, dry months of summer are almost over when Uncle Lucius, Jonathan, and Daniel return to Cyrene. Our uncle sent a message from Jerusalem saying they would be delayed and would not return immediately after the Festival of Pentecost, but he did not give us a reason.

Alexander and I see them on the day they arrive. As Uncle Lucius and his friends come up the hill from Apollonia, we run down the street to welcome them. Uncle Lucius hugs us, and then the three of them hurry off to their homes to let their families know they have finally arrived from Jerusalem.

Late that afternoon, Uncle Lucius comes to see our mother and father. Alexander and I listen to their conversation.

Uncle Lucius begins, "Daniel, Jonathan, and I gathered just outside the temple with a large crowd of people to begin our celebration of the Festival of Pentecost when a most amazing event occurred. It was unbelievable! I could hardly grasp what happened! If I had not been there to witness it myself, I would not believe it. A crowd of several thousand people from all over the Mediterranean world were gathered to celebrate Pentecost when there was the sound of rushing wind blowing all around us. There were some people there who, we soon learned, are followers of Jesus of Nazareth. He is the one you helped when you carried his cross, Simon. There were flames like the fire on the burning bush that appeared over each of them. They began to talk with us in the different languages of the people there. It was a miracle, a miraculous event created by the Holy Spirit. And what a wonderful happening it was! Then one of them, a man named Peter who was a disciple of Jesus, stood up to preach."

Uncle Lucius is absolutely aglow at this point, and he talks rapidly and with great excitement. "Peter said these are the days Joel the prophet talked about when God would pour out his Holy Spirit upon the people and there would be signs given for the coming of God's kingdom. He told us that Jesus of Nazareth, who had done such good deeds and then was handed over to the authorities to be killed, fulfilled the plans God had for him. He was crucified and buried. But, and this is what is so amazing, Jesus did not remain in the tomb. God raised him from the dead!"

At this point Father interrupts his brother-in-law. "Lucius, I couldn't sleep that night after we saw the crucifixion, so in the middle of the night I got up, dressed, and went out to where the crosses were. The other two men were still hanging there; they had not yet died. But Jesus had been taken away. The soldier said that his followers had taken him down from the cross and put him in a nearby tomb. Perhaps he was not really dead when they removed him from the cross."

"Oh, he was dead, all right," responds Uncle Lucius. "One of the soldiers had thrust a spear into his side. He was dead. But now he lives. His disciples saw him alive. He met them in Jerusalem, in the room where they had celebrated Passover. He appeared twice to them. And this is the amazing thing. His disciples had shut and bolted the door, but Jesus suddenly just appeared before them. He didn't come through the door; he seemed to come through the wall. He showed the disciples the wounds on his hands and feet and in his side. Later he appeared to some other followers as well, and finally he appeared to a large crowd in Galilee. Then he ascended into heaven."

"I can't believe a story like that, Lucius. Did you see him?" asks Father.

"No, I wish I had. But I talked to many people who did see him alive after his crucifixion. I believe what they told us. Jonathan and Daniel believe too. We have become followers of Jesus. We are convinced Jesus is the Messiah God has promised."

"Now wait, Lucius," Father interrupts again, "the Messiah would never die on a cross. That fate is for people who are cursed by God. The Messiah would never be so weak and helpless."

"Simon, I know what we have been taught. But the whole experience was so convincing. We know it was a miracle from God. If you had been there, you would believe too. The three of us were baptized, and in our baptism the Holy Spirit came to us too. It's a wonderful feeling, Simon, to experience the power of the Holy Spirit in your life. Because Jesus was raised from the dead, he has defeated the power of death. And if death has been defeated, all the other powers that can possibly harm us have been put down as well. Now I am really confident that God is with me, that God will guide me, and that God will save me from anything that might harm me. That is the power of the Holy Spirit."

"Lucius, I can see that what happened at Pentecost has really changed you," continues Father, "but it seems to me that dying on a cross is a sign of weakness, not victory."

"He is not dead, Simon. He has won the victory over death, and that is a greater victory than defeating the Roman legions. He *is* our Messiah," affirms Lucius with great emphasis.

"I don't know, Lucius, it all seems like some myth to me. How can you be so sure?"

"I saw it, Simon. I saw it with my own eyes, and I heard it all with my own ears. God sent the Holy Spirit that we might believe. I wish you could have seen and heard it, too. Tomorrow I will come back, and I'll bring Jonathan with me. You know how skeptical he can be. Maybe when he tells you about Jesus and what happened at Pentecost, you will be able to believe that Jesus is the Messiah.

With that Lucius arises to leave. "Shalom, Simon and Miriam; until tomorrow."

10

―――∿⚬◦⚬⚬◦∿―――

LUCIUS

The next evening I return to talk with Simon and Miriam. Jonathan is with me. The boys are home, but they are in another room studying their school lessons. The four of us gather around a table in the courtyard of Simon and Miriam's home. I know what is bothering Simon as I start our conversation.

"Simon, I spent a lot of time in the few days after Pentecost struggling with the idea that a person who was crucified could possibly be the Messiah. We have been taught in our Law that anyone who is executed and hung on a tree is cursed by God. But the miracle of the wind and tongues of fire was so compelling that I know God is at work in this new Jesus movement. But I, too, had trouble with the idea of a suffering messiah."

At the mention of messiah, Rufus sneaks back into the room to sit along the wall and listen to what we are saying.

"I did also," adds Jonathan. "We've been taught from the time we have been young children that the Messiah will be a victorious king who will again establish the kingdom of Israel as it was under King David. We have had that drummed into our minds from the day we entered synagogue school. After we were baptized as Jesus' followers, Lucius, Daniel, and I spent many days talking and studying. We discussed this with Jesus' disciples, who were working day and night to instruct all the new converts about what faith in Jesus really means. They directed us back to the prophets."

"But the prophets say the Messiah will be a great king like David," declares Simon.

"Well, some of the prophets say that," I respond, "but Jesus' disciples showed us that some of the prophecies about the Messiah have a different emphasis. They began with that passage in the prophet Isaiah about the Suffering Servant. You know what it says, Simon. Isaiah said that the appearance of this servant was marred so badly that he did not even appear to be human. He was despised and rejected, a man of great suffering. You saw Jesus, Simon, and I did too. Doesn't that describe what you saw when that soldier pulled you out to carry his cross?"

"Yes, of course it does," agrees Simon. "They had beaten him so severely; there was absolutely nothing at all appealing about his appearance, except for his eyes. If it had not been for the kindness in his eyes and a certain confidence I felt he had, I could not have even looked at him."

"And that is the point," Jonathan interjects. "Isaiah said that he was taken away by an unjust act and was cut off from the land of the living."

I break in again. "Isaiah tells us why this man had to suffer. His life was an offering for sin just like the offering of a sacrificial lamb on the altar. 'He was wounded for our transgressions and crushed for our sins,' wrote Isaiah. Because he was punished, we are made whole. We have sinned, but he has carried our sins to the cross, and now our sins are forgiven.

"That's the good news, Simon! We don't need to feel like we have lost favor with God when we disobey an edict in the Torah. Because of the suffering Jesus endured, we are forgiven. Jesus is like the Passover lamb that was killed so our people could leave slavery in Egypt. Jesus died so we may be set free from our slavery to sin, making it possible for us to live joyfully and triumphantly through the power of the Holy Spirit. Jesus gives us life that is abundant. He has overcome all the powers of evil that might harm us. Because of what he has done, we are free from fear. Nothing is able to harm us. You see, Jesus won a spiritual victory; his kingdom is spiritual, not political."

"I can see how excited you are about your new faith," Miriam observes, "and certainly the description of the Suffering Servant in Isaiah matches what Simon has told me about Jesus. But how does that qualify him as the Messiah?"

"Miriam, we have always believed the Messiah will conquer all the lands in the world and establish a kingdom of peace and prosperity. It took a while for me to come to the point where I realized Jesus really is triumphant. God raised him from the dead; that means he has conquered death. And if he has conquered death, the last enemy we humans experience, he is victorious over sin and evil too. The resurrection is the key to understanding this and believing Jesus is the Messiah. If he is alive, and I am convinced he is, then death has lost its power. We are free from the threat of death and from all that is evil.

Jonathan takes up the discussion again. "Look, Jesus came from the kingly line of David. David is his ancestor. In that sense he fulfills one of our expectations of the Messiah. Also, as we learned, he showed the wisdom of God in his teachings. He taught about righteousness and justice, and he encouraged people to repent from their sinful ways and do the will of God."

"Yes," I add, "and remember another passage Isaiah wrote. He said that the Messiah would come as a shoot from the stump of Jesse, that is, from David's father, and that the Spirit of the Lord would rest on him, the spirit of wisdom and understanding, the spirit of counsel and might, the spirit of knowledge and of the fear of the Lord. He will judge with righteousness and with equity and as a result of his teachings there will be peace on earth. Jesus has given us a new way to live."

"Simon and Miriam," continues Jonathan, "you know that teaching early in the book of the prophet Isaiah that the Lord's house will be elevated to the highest place, and all people will come to hear the word of the Lord. There God will teach us his ways, and as a result of his judgments, people will beat their swords into plowshares and their spears into pruning hooks, and they will not learn war any more. That is what Jesus has accomplished. In his teachings he has brought to us the wisdom and the knowledge of God. He has shown us how to live peaceably with one another and with all people in the world. That is the kingdom Jesus came to establish—a peaceable kingdom. His kingdom is not like Rome's kingdom exercising political power. His kingdom is a spiritual kingdom, and when his followers obey God, his kingdom comes near to us."

Jonathan and I have been talking so enthusiastically that we do not realize how much time has gone by. Simon glances down at Rufus. He is sound asleep on the floor. Simon goes over and picks him up to take him to bed. Miriam arises to go with him to tuck Rufus in and to get Alexander off to bed as well.

I realize that we have said enough for one night. We approach the doorway of the boys' room and quietly say, "Shalom." There will be time enough to continue our conversations about Jesus some other evening.

11

SIMON

M iriam always helps me process my thoughts, so when the boys are asleep and we retire to our room, I ask her a leading question, "What do you think about all Lucius and Jonathan said this evening concerning Pentecost and their becoming followers of Jesus?"

Miriam doesn't answer my question directly but continues our conversation with this observation, "When you met Jesus and helped him He made a very deep impression on you, didn't he? I wish I could have seen this Jesus the way you did, Simon."

"I wish you could have been there too. I don't know what it was about him that so touched me. At first I thought it was his eyes, the kindness and compassion I saw in them despite the intense pain and suffering he was enduring. If I had been in his position, an innocent man condemned to die, I would have been filled with rage.

"But as I reflect on it more, I realize it was not just the expression in his eyes that impressed me. He had a certain confidence and hope as he struggled along that road. It's like he put his terrible suffering in God's hands and knew that God would help him. That, it seems, gave him a sense of peace in the midst of the terrible pain he was experiencing. I don't know. There was just something about him that set him apart from everyone else.

"The soldiers obviously had the upper hand. The people along the road took one look at that awful spectacle and quickly moved on to do whatever else they had to do. They wanted no part in what was happening. If I had been able, I would have hurried on my way too, but that soldier forced me to carry Jesus' cross. And I am glad now that he did. Even though Jesus was weak from his beating, he had an inner strength that everyone else lacked. I still can't understand it; he was too weak to carry his cross, but at the same time he seemed to be stronger and more confident than any of the rest of us there that day."

"You said they put a sign above his head saying that he is the king of the Jews. Do you think that he is our king, Simon?"

"I wish I could answer that, Miriam. As Lucius and Jonathan were talking this evening, I was not surprised they are convinced Jesus is the Messiah. There certainly was something unique about him. What they reported concerning that event in Jerusalem at Pentecost seems to say that God is supporting and guiding this new movement. Something important must be happening because of Jesus. At this point I don't know what to think; I must hear more."

12

—⟿⟊⟑⟒⟒⟑⟊⟿—

LUCIUS

Several days go by before Jonathan and I can return to talk with Simon and Miriam. Daniel cannot join us this evening; he is discussing his faith in Jesus with his brother, Seth, and Seth's wife, Rachel. When we finally return to talk with Simon and Miriam, they are much more open to what we have to say about Jesus. Simon certainly had a significant experience in his encounter with Jesus on the way to the cross. It seems what we told him about Jesus the last time we were together changed his outlook. He is eager to get more information. In fact, he opens the discussion.

"I need to know more about Jesus. What kind of a man was he? What were his teachings all about? You said he did good works. Did he heal people? I saw a kind and compassionate man beaten and stumbling under the weight of a cross, yet a man who seemed confident and at peace. What kind of a person was he really?"

"Well, I can only tell you what other people have said about him," I respond. "He was a healer; there were a number of people we talked with in Jerusalem whom Jesus healed of different ailments. They said he was kind and compassionate. He taught that God is a loving God who cares for people and really wants people to understand that he is with them to help in every experience they have.

"Jesus used stories to teach people. I think the story he told that gives a clear picture of God's great love for us is a story about a father who had two sons. The younger son wanted to leave home to make his own way in the world, so he asked his father for his share of the inheritance that would come to him. His father gave it to him, and off he went."

"Now why would a father do a stupid thing like that?" interrupts Simon. "That makes no sense at all. I would never give Alexander or Rufus their inheritance while I am still alive."

"I'm sure you wouldn't, Simon. But that is what God does for all of us. He freely gives us life, the earth to grow our crops, and many other good gifts."

"And," adds Miriam, "God has given us two wonderful sons."

"As you might guess," I continue, "the younger son soon squandered all his money. He ended up feeding pigs to stay alive. At that point, he decided he would be better off if he returned home to ask his father to let him be one of the servants in his household. As he was coming up the road, his father saw him, ran out and embraced him, gave him fine clothing, and invited all his friends to come and celebrate his return."

"That is completely unrealistic. I would never do that," says Simon. "I would teach that boy a lesson he would never forget."

"Oh, Simon," responds Miriam, "you're so soft hearted. If either Alexander or Rufus did something like that, you would welcome them too. You might not throw a party, and you would complain to me for a week or two, but you would welcome either one of them with open arms."

"Well," I say, trying to complete my point, "that is the way God loves us. Even when we do something bad, God forgives us and welcomes us when we return to him."

"Yes," says Jonathan, "and remember the rest of the story. The older brother who stayed home and faithfully served his father came in from the fields while the 'welcome home' celebration was going on. When he found out his father welcomed home his errant brother with a party, he was angry, really angry. 'I have been faithful all of these years and you never gave me a party,' he said, and then he stalked off. But his father loved the older brother too."

"I think the lesson we learn from that story," I conclude, "is that God loves us even when we do not do what he wants. He wants us to return to him, and when we do, he welcomes us home."

"From this story it sounds like Jesus portrays God as a very permissive father; we can do anything we want and God will still accept and welcome us," says Simon. "I have always believed in a God of justice and righteousness, a God who judges and who punishes us when we do not obey the Law."

"We must be clear, Simon. Jesus did not teach us that we may do anything we want to do," Jonathan says. "He taught people that they have to be more righteous than the scribes and Pharisees, and you know how strict those people are in following the Law. What I see in Jesus is an emphasis on a new relationship with God. We do what is right not because we fear God will punish us but because we are grateful for what God has done for us in giving us Jesus. You don't want Alexander and Rufus to obey you simply because you will be angry and punish them if they disobey. You want them to obey you because they love you and are grateful for all you do to help them. I think that is the way it is with God. God does not want us to obey his commands simply because we are afraid he will punish us; he wants us to obey because we love him and are grateful for what he has done for us."

"Look, Simon," I continue, "there is another story Jesus told that may help you understand this a little better. There was a man who owed his master a tremendous amount of money. He could never have repaid it. His master was ready to throw him and his family into debtor's prison. This man begged his master to be merciful and forgive the debt, and amazingly, the master did. He left there no longer owing his master anything.

"On the way back to his home, the servant met a man who owed him a pittance, and he demanded payment. The man said he didn't have the money and begged his fellow-servant to give him a little more time to pay what he owed. His fellow-servant refused and had him thrown into debtor's prison. Word of what happened got back to the master. The master called the unmerciful servant in again. He condemned him to debtor's prison until the whole debt would be repaid, which means he would be there for the rest of his life. The point of this story is that God forgives us, but in turn we are to forgive other people when they offend us."

"So," summarizes Simon, "God loves us and is gracious and forgiving when we do what is wrong, but in return God expects us to love other people and to be gracious and forgiving toward them."

"That's right," I affirm. "And God demonstrated his wonderful love for us by giving us Jesus, who died on a cross. That's how much God loves each one of us. The cross is the sign of God's forgiving love."

"God loves all different people," breaks in Jonathan. "He didn't help just Jews; Jesus said God's concern extends to Samaritans and Gentiles too. He told a story about a man who was traveling between Jerusalem and Samaria. Robbers beat him and left him along the side of the road to die. A priest and a Levite walked by and did nothing to help the man. Then a Samaritan, an outsider we Jews will have nothing to do with, came along the road. He knelt down beside the man, lifted him onto his own donkey, and took him to an inn, where he could recover from his wounds. Jesus said this is the way we are to help one another. We are to love God with all our heart, soul, strength, and mind, and we are to love our neighbor as we love ourselves. Our neighbor is anyone we come in contact with who needs our help. And it doesn't matter who they are or where they have come from."

"That is really a hard thing to do," says Simon. "Are all his teachings as difficult as that?"

"Yes, some of them are very difficult," I reply. "It is not easy to follow Jesus. He calls us to a way of life that involves love, forgiveness, and humility. And that is just the opposite of what is natural for us. We are proud and self-centered; we resent it when other people offend or hurt us, and we want revenge. Jesus calls us to a different way of life that takes real discipline and effort. You have to be strong and courageous to follow Jesus. But that is the way God's kingdom comes on earth. It comes through the courageous efforts of the people who do his will."

Again time has slipped away very quickly. Simon and Miriam begin to yawn, and I realize it is time to stop our conversation for the evening. We bring our conversation to its conclusion and say, "Shalom."

When we leave, Simon invites us to return. "Jonathan, Lucius, please come again. I need to hear more about what Jesus taught."

We agree to return.

13

———⟡———

MIRIAM

"Simon, I have been listening to everything you and Lucius and Jonathan have been saying. I haven't said much because we women have been told by our rabbis that matters of faith and religious teachings should be left to men, but I must say that I find these teachings of Jesus to be very attractive. Think of it, Simon—God loves us. God loves us so much that he wants to welcome all of us into his presence. And when we come, he greets us with a party."

"It is a wonderful picture, but it runs against so much of what we have been taught," Simon cautions.

"I know. We have been taught that we must obey the Law, every little restriction laid down in it. And when we don't do what the Law says, God shows his displeasure by punishing us. When bad things happen, it's because we have disobeyed God. My mind is in a whirl.

"But do you know what I find most attractive and compelling about what Jesus taught? It is that we can trust God to be faithful to his promise to love us and care for us. When we are so confident of God's love, we realize that God acts in every event in life to work out what is good for us. We don't have to worry about what will happen in the future because we know God really loves us and will save us from harm. God wants us to love and serve him, but if we fall along the way, he still welcomes us when we come to him again. What a wonderful faith that is!"

"I hadn't thought about it quite that way, Miriam, but you have expressed it so well. I'm still having a little trouble figuring out how a loving God fits in with what I have always believed about a righteous and judgmental God. Our faith has taught us that God is righteous and just. God gave us the Law so we can know how to live to please him. I still think this new teaching makes God too permissive. I don't know, what do you think?"

"Well, I guess it's like Jonathan said about our relationship with Alexander and Rufus. We have certain rules in our home for the boys to follow. We love them very much, and when they break one of our rules, we expect them to say they are sorry. We may punish them in some way, but we always accept them back into our arms. And mostly they obey us because they want us to be pleased with what they do. We don't want Alexander and Rufus to obey us simply because they are afraid of us and what we might do to punish them. We want them to do the things we ask because they love us and want to please us. It seems to me that when we are convinced God loves us, we want to love and serve God in return. When we really love God, we will do what God commands. That's the way I see it, Simon."

"I think you are right, Miriam. What Lucius and Jonathan were emphasizing is that God loves and forgives us, so we should love and forgive each other. Something has really been bothering me since I got home from Jerusalem. I was so upset about the crucifixion scene, and I couldn't get it out of my mind. You know how I was when I got home. Well, on the voyage home, the men couldn't figure out why I was so depressed. Finally my good friend Isaac cornered me, and I explained what Lucius and I had seen and why I was so upset. He said, 'Oh come on, Simon, get over it. That fellow got what he deserved.' I got angry and flew back at him, cursing him. Isaac hasn't talked to me since. And we have always been such good friends."

"Simon, remember the story about the man who had been forgiven a huge debt but couldn't forgive the person who owed him so little," said Miriam. "God forgives you for cursing Isaac. Now you must go to Isaac to repair your relationship with him. Tomorrow morning find him and apologize; tell him you are sorry you spoke to him the way you did. I'm sure he will forgive you, just like God has forgiven you."

"I know. That is what Jesus would want me to do. I'll do it as soon as morning comes."

14

~~~ꞈꞈ꙳ꙮꙮ꙳ꞈꞈ~~~

SIMON

Early the next morning as the sun is just appearing over the hills in the east I leave our home to go out to the fields where I have just planted my next crop of wheat. As I round a bend in the road I see Isaac just ahead of me.

"Isaac," I call out, "please wait. I need to talk with you."

I don't know if he doesn't hear me or if he does not want to talk with me, because he keeps walking, head down watching the path in front of him.

"Isaac," I call again, louder this time.

He stops and turns half toward me. I hurry to catch up and we begin to walk side by side.

"Isaac," I begin, "I need to apologize for the way I treated you when we were on the boat coming back to Cyrene. I was so troubled, so depressed, by what I had witnessed that Friday after Passover. I was convinced that one man was innocent and I had never seen anyone being crucified before. It was horrible."

Isaac does not respond so I continue.

"When Rabbi Samuel said that this man, this Jesus, deserved to die because he had committed blasphemy I didn't say anything out of respect for our rabbi. Although now I wish I had spoken up then. But when you said the same thing on the boat I was just so frustrated and angry that I couldn't hold back my feelings. I am truly sorry for what

I said to you, for cursing you the way I did. You did not deserve that. I hope you will find it in your heart to forgive me, Isaac. We have been such good friends through the years and I don't want to lose your friendship."

There was more silence as we walked together. Finally, Isaac responded.

"Simon, of course I forgive you. I may have been out of line, too. Your depression was effecting all of us. We were all so excited about our journey to Jerusalem and the wonder of celebrating Passover there. Your depression was a damper on all the joy we felt. I simply wanted to shake you out of that dark place you were in. I thought I could do that by telling you to forget about that man whose cross you carried. I miscalculated. I did not understand how deeply your feelings ran concerning what you had witnessed. So I guess I need to apologize too."

Isaac put his arm around my shoulder and I knew that everything was right between us because of the forgiveness Jesus taught us to have. What a joy it is to have Isaac as a good friend again!

15

———⟡———

JONATHAN

"Lucius is busy this evening," I say as we gather around the table. "A mare went into labor, and Joseph has an appointment he cannot change. Lucius stayed with the mare to make sure she has no trouble delivering her colt."

"I know all about that," says Simon. "I don't have nearly as many horses as Lucius and Joseph have, but the mares always have a habit of delivering at the most inconvenient times. But Miriam and I are glad you are able to be here. I have so many questions. I think Miriam has some questions as well. For the most part Miriam has been sitting quietly listening to our conversation, but she has some things she could add. She and I talk quite a bit after you and Lucius leave."

"Well, Miriam, you would have found Jesus to be a wonderful friend. When we were in Jerusalem after Pentecost, we met many women who were followers of Jesus. Some of them supported the work he did with their gifts. He discussed matters of faith with women as well as men and taught them just as he taught the men who followed him. So please, Miriam, feel free to join our discussions."

"You and Lucius have talked a lot about God's love and mercy," Miriam begins, "and you said Jesus made it clear that he had not come to destroy the Law or what our prophets have taught us about justice and righteousness. Certainly Jesus must have said much more about these issues. It is very reassuring for us to know that God forgives our sins and loves us so much that he welcomes us even when we disobey him, but certainly God must have some standards of right and wrong. What did Jesus say about that?"

I pause a moment to organize my thoughts. "Let me begin this way, Miriam. You remember what the prophet Jeremiah said about a new covenant. He said that the day will come when God will make a new covenant with his people, a covenant that is different from the covenant he made with our ancestors at Mt. Sinai. He said God will put his Law within us and write it on our hearts.

"Jonathan," says Simon, "I think most of us Jews do have God's Law written in our hearts and minds. We don't always obey it, but we know what we should and should not do."

"Simon, the real difference is that in this new covenant, God says he loves us and that we are to love and obey him in return for all the good he does for us. God's commandments are written in our hearts and minds, and we obey God because we love him, not because we fear him. God's will becomes our will."

"I think I remember your saying Jesus taught that our righteousness is to exceed the righteousness of the scribes and Pharisees, the most upright people in our faith. What specifically did he say we should do to follow him?"

"Jesus said we are to love God with all of our being and that we are to love our neighbors as ourselves. He said we are to bless those who curse us and that we should love and pray for our enemies. If someone hits us on one cheek, we are not to strike back but rather turn the other cheek. If someone forces us to go a mile, we should go two miles.

"We should not be angry, because anger and hatred incline us to murder. We should not look with lust, because that may lead to fornication and adultery. And we should not covet what other people have because that tempts us to steal. We are to be so righteous that we exceed the commandments given on Mt. Sinai. Jesus said, too, that if we are angry with a brother or sister when we come to worship, we must first go and be reconciled to the one we are angry with, and then we may come back to worship with a pure heart. We must have a right relationship with people around us if we want to have a right relationship with God."

"That is so important," breaks in Simon. "Miriam and I were talking about that before we went to bed after your last visit. I told her that on the ship when we were returning home from Jerusalem, I got really angry with Isaac. I was so distraught over the scene at the crucifixion of Jesus, and Isaac said I should get over it because Jesus got what he deserved. I cursed him. We hadn't talked with each other since, and we had been such good friends. So the morning after I told Miriam about this, I caught up with Isaac on the way to our fields and told him how sorry I was that I had spoken that way. I asked him to forgive me, and he did. Now Isaac and I are good friends again, and I know God, too, has forgiven me for what I said to damage our friendship."

"See, his teachings do help us, don't they?" I reply.

"But that teaching bothers me a little," says Miriam. "When I take our flour to the market, sometimes mischievous boys kick dirt and stones in the bags of flour if I leave them uncovered. It really makes me angry when they do that. If I yell at them, they just laugh and run away. Then they will come back and do it all over again. I get so angry with them, I could beat them."

"Remember, Jesus said we should not retaliate against someone who harms us. Our Law says we may return an eye for an eye and a tooth for a tooth, but Jesus said if someone does something bad to us, we are not to retaliate. We are to return kindness to those who hurt us. If we do retaliate, take an eye for an eye, the conflict may escalate. They will come back and do something worse to us. But when we return good for evil, we defuse the conflict. I know that is very hard to do, but that is what Jesus taught us. He said we are to love our enemies and do what is good to those who harm us. In that way we create an opportunity for reconciliation that may lead to peace. When we live that way, we are bringing God's kingdom to earth."

"What else did Jesus teach us?" asks Miriam.

"Well," I continue, "he said we are always to tell the truth. There is no need for us to take an oath to tell the truth, because everything that comes out of our mouths is to be truthful. We should not lie."

At that Alexander sticks his head around the doorway and says, "You mean I have to tell Father and Mother when I get in trouble with Rabbi Samuel at school?"

"If they ask how things went at school, you need to tell the truth," I reply.

"I'm not sure I like that," says Alexander. "I always get into more trouble at home than I do at school. Father is stricter than Rabbi Samuel."

"Look," I respond, "why don't you and Rufus join us out here at the table? I guess you have been listening to our conversation; you might as well sit here and listen. Perhaps you will learn something from what we say, and you can ask your questions as well."

"Okay, come on Rufus. Rufus hasn't been doing his lessons; he's been listening to everything you have been saying."

"That's not true," protests Rufus. "I have been doing my lessons."

"You have not," replies Alexander.

"Now, boys, which one of you is really telling the truth?" I ask.

"Well, he has done a little work," admits Alexander, "but he has been listening more than working. And that's the whole truth."

"Okay, well join us here. Sit with me. Jesus told his followers that we are to be humble; Jesus said that is one of the more important characteristics for his followers. We are to be merciful. We have talked about how we are to forgive other people. We are to have pure hearts; that is, we are to love and serve God alone. One of the things I had a lot of difficulty understanding about his teachings is the whole matter of being meek and humble. That sounds so weak. It seems that if we are humble, we let other people push us around and walk all over us."

"Yes, that's what it sounds like to me too," Simon adds.

"When I really began to consider everything Jesus' disciples said about him, I realized that what he taught makes good sense. If we really believe God is faithful and fulfills all the promises he has made, then our strength comes to us from the Holy Spirit. We don't have to trust in our own strength and skill; we trust in the Spirit's strength and guidance. Then because we have that faith, we can be humble and merciful. Being humble and merciful is not a sign of our weakness; it is a sign of God's strength and the power God gives us through the Holy Spirit."

"At school," Alexander says, "Jacob is a bully. He is always pushing people around and making trouble for all of us. Do you mean I shouldn't push him back? Am I just to let him get away with it when he is mean to me?"

"That's what Jesus would have you do," I respond. "And I bet if you do that a couple of times, he may stop bullying you. It's no fun to bully people when they don't do anything to retaliate."

"I don't know," says Alexander. "It doesn't sound to me like a good way to handle a bully."

"Well, try it sometime, Alexander, and let me know what happens. It's getting late. You boys need to get to bed. Perhaps we should stop our conversation for tonight so all of us can get the rest we need for tomorrow."

"Thanks for coming by," Simon says as we get up from the table. "You have given us a lot to think about. I really am beginning to believe I want to be a follower of Jesus too. Shalom, Jonathan"

"Good," I respond as we walk to the door. "Lucius and I will come again in a day or two to talk some more about the faith we have in God because of what Jesus has done. Shalom, Simon and Miriam. Shalom, boys."

16

———⟋⟍⟋⟍⟋⟍———

MIRIAM

Lucius is my baby brother, younger by six years. We have an older brother, Joseph, who is married to Sarah, and they have a little boy. Joseph has run the stables since our father died in that storm at sea. He and Lucius and the men they employ raise horses and sell many of them to military companies in Rome. They travel back and forth to Rome with a boatload of horses at least once a year. I'm always very anxious when they make that trip, and you can certainly understand why. I lost my father in a storm at sea; I don't want to lose my brothers as well.

Our father was the one who built up the stable of horses. He got started in his business when the demand for horses in the Roman military was increasing, and he rode the wave of that demand to build a very profitable business breeding and raising horses here in Cyrene. Joseph has continued that tradition; our family has been very successful.

Lucius, however, does not share the passion for this business that Joseph has. He does his share of the work, but his heart is not in it. Lucius is a contemplative person. He spends a lot of time thinking and debating philosophical and religious issues. A year or so ago he talked with Rabbi Samuel about going to Jerusalem to study to be a rabbi. I can understand why he has become so passionate about Jesus and his teachings. It is really in his nature to be a religious teacher and leader.

Lucius and Jonathan have been talking about faith in Jesus with Joseph and Sarah and our mother too. Jonathan also has convinced his wife, Naomi, that she should become a follower of Jesus.

At the end of the week following the Sabbath service, Lucius and Jonathan ask all of us to gather in the square in front of the synagogue.

Lucius speaks first: "I understand all of you are interested in following Jesus." We all indicate that we are. "So," Lucius continues, "we need to gather to discuss the next step we should take as followers of Jesus."

Jonathan then issues an invitation, "Please come to our home tomorrow evening. Naomi will prepare a simple meal for us, and Lucius, Daniel, and I will tell you what we believe should be the next thing we do. Jesus said that we are to baptize new believers and tomorrow evening we will talk about what that means and how we will do the baptisms. In addition, we should begin to meet regularly on the first day of the week. The followers of Jesus who are in Jerusalem meet for worship and fellowship on the first day of the week because that is the day Jesus was raised from the dead. They celebrate the resurrection on the day after our Jewish Sabbath." We all agree we will be at Jonathan and Naomi's home the next evening.

When we gather the following evening we greet one another and then take our places around a large table set in the center of their courtyard. Jonathan arises to begin our meal. He offers a prayer of thanksgiving: "God our Father, we thank you for sending Jesus into the world to be our Savior. As he died on the cross to save us, may we be dead to sin and be raised with him to new life. By your Holy Spirit, give us the strength we need to follow Jesus in your way. Amen."

After the prayer, Jonathan takes a loaf of bread that is on a plate before him. Jonathan explains that the believers in Jerusalem break bread as Jesus did in the last Passover meal he had with his disciples. Jesus said that this bread was his body broken for all. Then at the end of the meal, Jesus took a cup of wine and said this was his blood shed for people's sins. By breaking bread at the beginning of the meal, we recognize the presence of the risen Christ at our holy supper. Then

Jonathan breaks the loaf. Each of us takes a piece from the loaf and eats it. Then Naomi brings the food and places it on the table.

After we have eaten, Lucius talks about what commitment to Jesus really means and says if we want to follow him, we need to be baptized. We all question him about what baptism signifies. He explains, "The water of baptism is a sign of our being cleansed from sin. When believers sincerely repent and are baptized, they come out of the water free from sin. Through the power of the Holy Spirit, someone who is baptized becomes a new person, a person who is transformed, made new, and set apart as a follower of Jesus the Messiah!

"Baptism also is the rite of initiation into a new way of life, life in the kingdom of God. In baptism believers give up their old way of life, a life of selfishness and sin, and begin a new way of life, a life of obedience to the teachings of Jesus the Messiah. Through the power of the Holy Spirit, those who are baptized become part of life in the new community of faithful people committed to Jesus. He said that we are to be baptized in the name of the Father and of the Son and of the Holy Spirit. The disciples of Jesus said baptism should take place in living water—that is, water that is flowing. If no living water is available, then we can pour out water three times upon the head of the person being baptized." Lucius goes on to say that he thinks the water of the Mediterranean Sea qualifies as living water so we can go down to the coastline at Apollonia to be baptized.

I am amazed at how confident my little brother has become as a leader in our fellowship. He really is a changed person, more confident, more self-assured, and much more humble. He never was obnoxiously proud, but he sometimes had a chip on his shoulder. Now that has disappeared through the power of the Holy Spirit. He really is a new person in Christ.

When we hear what we should do, we all agree that we are interested in being baptized so we can begin our new lives as followers of Jesus Christ.

We decide that on the next Sabbath, after worship at the synagogue we will go to the shore just outside of Apollonia to be baptized. Then we will gather the next day, the Lord's Day, to share another sacred meal. This time we will meet at Lucius's home, and Joseph and Sarah will be our host and hostess.

After we are finished eating, Jonathan again stands and raises a cup of wine. He says the wine represents the blood of Christ that was shed for us and for all his followers. Then we pass the cup, and each of us drinks a bit of the wine. Then Jonathan closes our meal with a prayer of blessing.

Simon, our boys, and I are very happy that we have made our commitment to follow Jesus. We certainly do not know how things will work out in the years ahead, but we are sure God will be our strength, Jesus will be our Savior, and the Holy Spirit will be our guide and helper.

17

———∿∿◦◦⌒◦◦⌒◦◦∿∿———

JONATHAN

After our worship service the next Sabbath, we gather in front of the synagogue to walk down the road to Apollonia. There are sixteen of us: Simon, Miriam, Alexander, and Rufus; Daniel along with his wife, Judith, and their young son; Daniel's brother, Seth, and his wife, Rachel; Joseph and Sarah and their son; Lucius and his mother, Rebekah; and my wife, Naomi, and me.

We assemble at a beach outside the city along the Mediterranean Sea. I begin by offering a prayer: "Lord God Almighty, we give thanks that you have called us to be followers of Jesus the Messiah and that you have shown your love by freely offering us forgiveness and new life through his death and resurrection. As these new believers enter the waters of baptism we pray that your Holy Spirit may come upon them so that they may come out of the water clean and free from the power of sin. We pray that they may lay aside their former way of life so they may become people of your kingdom and members of your community of believers. We offer this prayer through our Lord Jesus Christ. Amen."

Then Daniel asks several questions of the thirteen who have come to be baptized: "Do you believe Jesus is the Messiah, and do you accept him as your Lord and Savior?

We answer, "Yes, we believe that Jesus is the Messiah, our Lord and our Savior."

"And do you promise to follow his teachings and do his will, and will you faithfully serve him as long as you live?"

Again we affirm our faith, "We do."

Then Lucius, Daniel, and I take each person individually into the water. We immerse the new believers, baptizing them in the name of the Father and of the Son and of the Holy Spirit. Some small children are afraid to go under the water, so we take them in our arms and pour some water three times on their heads. After everyone has been baptized, we gather on the shore and each of us prays that the Holy Spirit may inspire and help us to be faithful to the promises that we made. The prayers are fervent and sincere, and although there is no sound of rushing wind and no tongues of fire, we know the Holy Spirit truly is present and that each new believer will be a faithful follower of Jesus. With our spirits lifted by the joy that fills our hearts, we chant a psalm.

> What shall I return to the Lord for all his bounty to me?
> I will lift up the cup of salvation and call on the name of
> the Lord. I will pay my vows to the Lord in the presence of
> all his people. Precious in the sight of the Lord is the death
> of his faithful ones. O Lord, I am your servant; I am your
> servant, the child of your serving girl. You have loosed my
> bonds. I will offer to you a thanksgiving sacrifice and call
> on the name of the Lord. I will pay my vows to the Lord in
> the presence of all his people.[10]

Then we retrace our steps back up the road to our homes in Cyrene.

The next evening we gather again on the Lord's Day, this time at Joseph and Sarah's home. We begin our meal as we did at our first meeting, with a prayer of thanksgiving and the breaking of bread, receiving it in the name of the Messiah and thereby recognizing the presence of the risen Christ at our table. Now we truly feel we are a fellowship of believers and that in the breaking of the bread and the passing of the cup, Christ truly is present in our fellowship.

After we have finished eating, I tell the story Jesus told about the prodigal son and the waiting father. At the conclusion of the story I add,

"Jesus told this story so that everyone who believes in him may know that God loves each one of us like parents love their children."

This comment creates a lot of discussion. All the people, even the children, join in with their comments.

"I've always believed in a God of judgment, a God who is to be feared if we disobey the commandments. It really is different believing in a God who loves us."

"If we do what is wrong God welcomes us back as one of his children. God loves us even more than parents love their children. If one of my children did what that boy did I wouldn't be so quick to welcome him home and I certainly wouldn't give him a party when he returned."

"I'm going to have to change my way of thinking about God. A loving God is so much different from a judgmental God."

"I can hardly believe that I am a child of God and that God welcomes me into his presence."

People truly were beginning a understand what Jesus came to teach us about God.

As we close our discussion, Lucius makes an announcement about his future plans: "I am going to return to Jerusalem to learn more about Jesus from the disciples. I will leave very soon, before the winter storms increase the risk of travel by sea. But you will be in good hands. Jonathan and Daniel will stay here in Cyrene to be the leaders of our group of believers."

Then we pass the cup as we did at our meeting a week ago and close our time together with prayer. Each one of us has the opportunity to offer a prayer, and most of us do so; even the children say a prayer to God. Many of us ask God to give Lucius safe passage to Jerusalem. I can tell that Rebekah, Lucius's mother, and Miriam are upset by the news that he is returning to Jerusalem. They have tears in their eyes when they hug their son and brother. I am sure, however, that they know Lucius has important work ahead of him, and while they will miss him, they will support him in any way they can.

Cyrene
November, AD 30

18

—⦿⦿⦿⦿⦿—

SIMON

Aweek or two after our baptism Miriam asks me, "Simon, have you talked with your brother Caleb about what happened in Jerusalem and the faith we now have in Jesus as the Messiah?"

"No," I reply, "but we really ought to get together with them to tell them everything that has happened. They probably are wondering why Lucius has left so suddenly for Jerusalem. Caleb and I are going to work together at his farm tomorrow, and I'll ask him if we can spend an evening with him and Esther. Perhaps we can go to their home tomorrow evening."

The next day I tell Caleb that Miriam and I have something we want to discuss with Esther and him, that we would like to come over that evening. He readily agrees to have us come after our evening meal.

When Miriam and I arrive, we talk about our farm work and catch up on what each other's children are doing. I guess I am a little nervous about telling the story of what happened to me in Jerusalem when I carried Jesus' cross and our belief now that he is our long-awaited Messiah.

Finally I begin. "Caleb and Esther, we have something very important to talk about with you this evening—something that has brought a real change in our lives."

First I tell them what happened to me in Jerusalem when I was singled out from the crowd to carry the cross of a man who was about to be crucified. They are horrified that a person who was so obviously innocent would be nailed to a cross to die. "But," I continue, "That is not the end of the story."

Then Miriam breaks into the conversation. She tells them what happened to her brother, Lucius, and his friends when they celebrated Pentecost in Jerusalem. She emphasizes that they were attracted by the signs they saw of God's Holy Spirit in that crowd of people and then were convinced by the preaching of one of Jesus' disciples that he had been raised from the dead to be the Messiah all of us Jews are expecting.

Then I pick up the story again and tell my brother and sister-in-law everything that happened here in Cyrene since Lucius, Jonathan, and Daniel returned from Jerusalem.

Miriam and I rush along so rapidly with our account of all that took place that we give no time for Caleb or Esther to ask any questions. Finally, when we come to the end of our story, there is complete silence in the room. Caleb and Esther seem to be dumbfounded by everything we have said. I realize we have told them so much that they cannot digest it all at once. Perhaps they think we are off on some wild chase after another false messiah. Finally they look at one another, and then Caleb speaks. His reaction is much the same as Miriam and mine had been. "How could someone who was crucified be the Messiah? Our Messiah will be a triumphant and victorious person."

We explain what Isaiah said about the Suffering Servant and how Jesus suffered and died as the sacrifice for our sins. We reiterate that Jesus has made us whole and explain that through his teachings, he has shown us the way to enter God's kingdom.

We realize we have said more than they could absorb in one evening, so we invite them to come to our home soon so we may answer the questions they have about our testimony concerning Jesus. They agree.

We get together several more evenings, and on the fourth meeting, Jonathan comes to explain what belief in Jesus really involves. Their main question has to do with the Law—the Torah. Jonathan explains to them that Jesus did not come to do away with the Law but to fulfill it. He tells them about Jesus' teachings concerning lust and anger and hatred and divorce and how all of his teachings on these subjects exceed the requirements of the Law. He goes on to say that even when we are guilty of any of these sins, we know we will be forgiven. The Law indicates to us what is right and what is wrong, but even when we do what is wrong, God forgives us because of the sacrifice of Jesus on the cross.

That evening we invite Caleb and Esther to come to our meetings on the Lord's Day so they can hear more about faith in Jesus and what he taught his disciples. Not too many weeks go by before Caleb and Esther decide they, too, will become followers of Jesus. Soon they are baptized.

19

─────〰〜◦୧୨◦〜〰─────

ALEXANDER

The next spring, after Passover, Uncle Lucius makes his first trip back to Cyrene from Jerusalem. He reports to our small group that the community of believers in Jerusalem is growing very rapidly. He tells us stories of the healings Peter and John and other disciples have performed and how these healings have brought new growth in the number of Jesus' followers.

He tells us, too, about some problems that are developing. The high priest and the council in Jerusalem are beginning to oppose this new movement. A few of the leaders in the church at Jerusalem have been arrested and jailed. Some of the people there are afraid that this opposition will soon grow and all of the followers of Jesus will be in danger of persecution. Uncle Lucius says he hopes this persecution will not come to Cyrene but that we should be prepared to defend our faith in Jesus. We all affirm that we certainly will remain faithful to Jesus whatever might happen.

After a brief visit with his mother and the other members of his family, Uncle Lucius returns to Jerusalem. He is convinced God has some special work for him to do there, and he wants to learn as much as he can about Jesus and his teachings.

About the time Uncle Lucius leaves for Jerusalem, some rabbis from Judea arrive in Cyrene to meet with Rabbi Samuel. We do not know what they talk about, but right after they leave, Rabbi Samuel begins to be less friendly with Father and Mother and the other people in our small group of believers.

At our synagogue school Rabbi Samuel is beginning to teach more and more about what the prophets have written concerning the Messiah. Today he said, "The Messiah will come sometime in the future. He will be a great leader who will raise a mighty army that will defeat the Roman legions. When the Messiah has driven the Romans from our land people will come to Jerusalem as Isaiah has told us. Then all nations will come to Mt. Zion to learn the will of the Lord. They will beat their swords into plowshares and their spears into pruning hooks and everyone in the world will enjoy peace and prosperity. There are false messiahs who have tried to defeat the Romans and have failed. These so-called messiahs have not brought the justice and righteousness of God's kingdom. When the true Messiah comes we will know beyond the shadow of a doubt that God has sent him."

I talk with Father and Mother about what the rabbi is teaching us, and they tell Rufus and me that we should just be quiet about what we believe concerning Jesus being the Messiah and accept what Rabbi Samuel teaches without any comment. It is hard for us to do this because we know Jesus is the Messiah, but we do what our parents advise us to do.

Then something happens that makes Rabbi Samuel become more firm in his teachings in the synagogue school and in our Sabbath worship. Our little group of believers begins to grow. Ruth, who is Father's good friend Isaac's wife, takes sick. She is vomiting and has a high fever. After two days, Isaac is worried almost to the point of panic, and he asks Father what we can do.

Immediately Father contacts Jonathan, and the two of them ask our entire band of believers to gather at Isaac and Ruth's home. Within an hour, we assemble there. We pray for Ruth in the name of Jesus and ask God to heal her. Jonathan lays hands on her and prays that the evil spirit that is making her sick will come out of her. In about an hour, Ruth begins to improve. Her fever comes down; she stops vomiting. The next morning she is well. Through our prayers and the laying on of hands, God has healed Ruth. We all rejoice at what God has done.

Isaac and Ruth and their two children begin to come to our meetings. After they learn more about Jesus, what he did, and what he taught, they decide they want to be baptized and become followers of Jesus. After Sabbath worship at the end of that week, we all go down to the seashore at Apollonia, where Isaac, Ruth, and their children are baptized.

The news about Ruth's healing quickly spreads among the people in our synagogue. People begin to ask Rabbi Samuel about the new group that has formed. They question him about what they have heard concerning Jesus. They want to know why there are some people in the synagogue who are meeting on the day after the Sabbath.

Rabbi Samuel believes that our little group is becoming a threat to the unity of his congregation and to the purity of the Jewish faith. He notifies Jonathan and our father that he wants to meet with them. We don't know what was said in that meeting except that Jonathan and Father assure the rabbi that it is the intention of all the people in our group to continue to attend services in the synagogue, send their children to the synagogue school, and in every way be good Jews. Rabbi Samuel apparently tells them that they cannot be good Jews while they believe Jesus is the Messiah. That is all we know about their conversation.

Soon we see that many people in the synagogue are turning against us. People no longer speak to our families after the service is over. When we meet other members of the synagogue in the street or in the marketplace, they turn away. Some of them stop buying the flour Mother sells in the market. We are being shunned by the people who have been our friends. It is difficult to take.

In our meetings, Jonathan emphasizes that we have to continue to be kind to the people who are turning against us. We should smile and greet them when we meet them on the street or in the marketplace. We should never turn away from them even though they will not speak to us. One of Mother's good friends, Joanna, cannot break off her relationship with Mother. She keeps in touch with Mother, and she even comes to one of our meetings to see what all this Jesus stuff, as her husband, Matthew, calls it, is about. She warns Mother that the leaders in the synagogue are planning to take more drastic steps to oppose us and that if we do not give up our belief that Jesus is the Messiah, we might be prohibited from attending worship on the Sabbath.

We are not about to change our minds about Jesus. We really believe Jesus is the Messiah, and we intend to profess publically that Jesus is Lord. A couple of weeks later, Rabbi Samuel tells Father, Jonathan, and the other men in our group that their children are no longer permitted to come to school at the synagogue. We, along with all the other children in our group of believers, are expelled. Jonathan begins to teach us, and he teaches us about Jesus along with the Torah and the other parts of our Scriptures. We like our new classes because Jonathan is a much better teacher than Rabbi Samuel.

20

———∿∿◦◠◡◯◦◯◯◡◦◦∿∿———

JONATHAN

I n the years immediately after Rabbi Samuel received that visit from the rabbis in Jerusalem and expelled our children from the synagogue school, he has become much more adamant that those of us who believe Jesus is the Messiah are a threat to the Jewish faith. We do not consider ourselves enemies of Judaism. We continue to attend synagogue worship, and we celebrate all the holy days of our faith. We have just added to our Jewish beliefs the teachings of Jesus, and we believe those teachings in no way contradict the Torah or the teachings of the prophets. In fact, Jesus' teachings support the Law and the prophets. But the pressure against us is becoming more pronounced as time passes.

There is social pressure. The ties our people have with other members of the synagogue have begun to fray. Even good friends are starting to pull away from one another. When we go to services in the synagogue, people shun us. When we greet them, they do not return our greeting. I have always been good friends with Nathan, a fellow teacher, but now he turns his back on me. Rabbi Samuel and the leaders of the synagogue continually speak of us as enemies of the true faith of Judaism and followers of a notorious heretic. Rabbi, in his sermons, teaches more and more about what he considers the false teachings of Jesus. Why can they not see that Jesus' teachings are no threat to the truth of our Jewish faith? How can they be so blind that they consider

Jesus a false prophet? It makes no sense to me. The congregation at the synagogue is being torn apart.

There is economic pressure too. Simon and Miriam are not able to sell as much flour as they have previously at the market. Customers they have served for years now go to other farmers to buy their flour. The same is true for Isaac and Ruth. Our good friends are suffering.

We talk about this when we meet on the Lord's Day. We have determined that even though our friends are turning against us and we are losing income in the process, we will not retaliate in any way. Above all else, we will not turn away from the faith we have in Jesus.

Lucius came home to Cyrene to visit us a month ago. He said the situation for the followers of Jesus in Jerusalem is much worse than it is here in Cyrene.

He reported, "Followers of the Way are being thrown into prison. One of the leaders in the Jerusalem congregation, a man named Stephen, who had been appointed a deacon to help to care for those who have need, was actually stoned to death when he dared to defend his faith in Jesus. That started a terrible round of persecution in Jerusalem, and the believers are beginning to move out of the city to Samaria and to other villages and cities in the area. There they are witnessing to the truth about Jesus, and the movement now is expanding in those areas too.

"One of the wonderful things God has done, however, is that a young rabbi named Saul, who was particularly active in persecuting followers of Jesus, has been converted. He and some men with him were on the way to Damascus to round up followers of Jesus to imprison them when a most amazing thing happened! He had a vision. The risen Messiah, Jesus himself, appeared to him and spoke, asking why Saul was persecuting him. Saul was blinded, and the men with him led him into Damascus, where the followers of Jesus in that city came to him. His sight was restored, and he began to preach about Jesus there in Damascus. The Jewish authorities in Damascus tried to capture Saul, but he escaped and traveled back to Jerusalem. There he carried on a debate with the Hellenist Jews, declaring to them the truth about Jesus. They tried to kill him, so the believers in Jerusalem hastily got him away from the city and sent him on to his home in Tarsus."

When we hear how bad things are in Jerusalem and in Judea, we realize that what we are experiencing is mild compared to what others are enduring. We thank Jesus for that.

Lucius was in a hurry to go back to Jerusalem. He said there was so much work to do there. The movement is growing very rapidly, and they need all the help they can find. Lucius believes he will be sent to Antioch, where a new group of believers is forming.

We all went down to Apollonia to bid farewell to Lucius. Before he boarded the ship that would take him to Joppa, we prayed for his safe journey and for the success of his work in Jerusalem or Antioch or wherever else he may serve.

When we meet on the next Lord's Day, we talk about how uncomfortable we feel worshiping in the synagogue. We decide we will stop attending worship at the synagogue and instead meet for worship on the Lord's Day. We will begin our worship with a psalm of praise and a prayer. Then one of our leaders, Jonathan or Daniel, will read lessons from the Torah and the prophets and teach us what these words mean for us as followers of Jesus. Then we will have a time for confession. Following that we will break the bread and receive the cup and then eat our sacred meal. After the meal, there will be a time for individual prayers, and then we will sing another psalm and end our time together by affirming our faith using a statement of belief Lucius has given to us.

> We believe in God the Father almighty, and we believe in Jesus Christ, his Son. We believe Jesus was crucified and that God raised him from the dead. We believe in the Holy Spirit, whom God sent to give us strength and help as we live. Jesus is Lord. He forgives our sins and gives us life that is eternal. Amen.

21

~~w•๏•๛๏•๏•๏๏~~

ALEXANDER

Years have passed since we became believers in Jesus. I am now a young man, and my little brother, Rufus, is fifteen years old. He's the smart one, and our elder, Jonathan, is teaching him so that in time he may become a leader in our group of believers. I work much more closely with our father sowing and reaping, taking care of the horses, and milling the wheat into flour. I enjoy my work on the farm, and I particularly appreciate the opportunity I have to hear Father talk about his trip to Jerusalem, his carrying the cross for Jesus, and what that means to him now that he believes Jesus is the Messiah. We often talk for hours about the faith we share. Then one day tragedy strikes our family.

About two years ago, one of our mares gave birth to a frisky little colt. The colt grew to be a high-spirited stallion. He has been hard to control. One terrible day, Father gets him out of his stall to lead him to the mill to be hitched to the pole that turns the top millstone as it grinds the grains of wheat into flour. The horse always balked at doing this. He didn't like being hitched to anything, and he particularly did not want to walk in circles all day turning that millstone.

Then comes that terrible day. When Father is leading him, really pulling him to the mill, suddenly the stallion rears up on his hind legs. Father slips on a patch of wet grass as he tries to get out of the way, and the horse comes crashing down on him, one front hoof hitting his chest and the other coming down on his abdomen. The horse breaks free and runs out into the field.

I realize immediately Father has very serious injuries. He cries out in pain. I gather him in my arms and carry him into the house, laying him on his bed. Mother is talking to our neighbor, Julia, and when I call out for help, Mother and Julia run into our home. They can see Father is very seriously injured. Rufus runs to get Jonathan, and soon our whole congregation is in our house.

Mother is crying. Julia comforts her. Jonathan and some other men remove Father's clothing and clean his wounds, but there is no way they can repair the damage done to his body.

Everyone prays for Father. The women gather around Mother to comfort her. Father is in such pain he can barely talk. I think he knows he is dying. Several hours go by. Julia's husband, Gaius, comes from his blacksmith shop to see what he can do. We tell him all he can do is pray for Father.

It is toward midday when Father begins to slip away. He goes into a coma. His breathing becomes more shallow and sporadic. We all know the end is coming. Jonathan leads us in a prayer that Father will have safe passage into Jesus' arms. Another half-hour or hour goes by; no one is counting the time.

Suddenly Father opens his eyes and looks straight up to the ceiling. He exclaims, "It's Jesus, the man whose cross I carried. He is reaching out his hand to take me with him into his kingdom." Father raises his right arm to grasp the hand of Jesus. His face glows with a smile as he takes the outstretched hand of the Lord. Then his arm falls back on the bed, his eyes close, and he stops breathing. Our father is dead. Mother breaks down sobbing. Rufus and I cling to each other. How can we go on without the one who has been our guide and our inspiration in life?

Jonathan leads us in a brief prayer. Several of the people prepare Father's body for burial. They wash, anoint, and bind his body with grave clothes and place it on a simple bier. We take Father's body to our cemetery, where his father and mother and other members of his family are buried. Jonathan leads us in a brief service in which we commit Father's body to the ground, ashes to ashes and dust to dust. But Father's spirit we commit to Jesus, where he will dwell in his Savior's kingdom forever.

22

———∿∾◦◝◦⊙◝◦∾◦∿———

GAIUS

J ulia and I go to the cemetery with the others to bury Simon's body. We are not Jews, and we do not share the faith of those who follow Jesus. We are only concerned friends and neighbors who are so very sorrowful that Simon has died. Julia and I have always admired Simon and Miriam. How could we not be impressed? Simon was such a good man; he and Miriam have been wonderful and loving people. They have never had anything bad to say about anyone. They have worked hard and have done what is right. I really feel sorry for Miriam, and I will certainly miss Simon.

When Julia and I return from Simon's burial, I tell her that I am intrigued by what had happened when Simon died. I ask Julia what I think is a very innocent question—a question that opens a very lengthy and illuminating discussion that goes on long into the evening.

"Julia, what do you think about what we saw today, particularly the vision it appears Simon had when he died? I don't know what to make of it. Do you?"

"No, I really don't. Miriam and I have talked a little about what she and Simon believe. As Jews they have always followed a very high moral code. The Jewish people we know here in Cyrene are all very good people. They have their Ten Commandments and the teachings in the Torah to guide them, and I have always admired the way they live their lives. But the vision Simon had at the end caught me completely by surprise. It was like the heavens opened to receive him."

"What did Simon mean when he made that statement about the man whose cross he carried?"

"Do you remember about ten years ago Simon went to Jerusalem with a group of men from the synagogue here in Cyrene? They went to celebrate one of their holy days; they call it Passover, I believe. It has something to do with the Jews being liberated from slavery in Egypt. Well, when Simon returned from that trip, Miriam was disturbed by the change that came over him. Miriam and I talked about what had happened. She told me that Simon had an unusual experience. He was called out of a crowd along the road to carry the cross of a person who was being led out of the city to be crucified. That made an indelible impression on him, and it troubled him very deeply. He believed the man was falsely accused."

"Well, why would he say that this person who was crucified is welcoming him to his kingdom? That doesn't make any sense at all to me. What kind of a king would a crucified criminal make?"

"Miriam has talked with me about their faith. It seems that her brother Lucius stayed in Jerusalem until another one of their holy days, and he became involved in a movement within Judaism. What I have been able to gather from her remarks is that this person whose cross Simon carried was a teacher who was innocent of any crime. His crucifixion was a miscarriage of justice. But what happened after he had been put in the tomb is what was so miraculous. They said that after he died, he appeared several times to his followers."

"You mean he was raised from the dead? I'm not sure I could ever accept such a tale."

"Well, if Simon really saw him and recognized him in that moment when he died, this teacher may well be alive. I mean, you were there as I was. We know what we saw and what we heard Simon say. Maybe this person, I think Miriam said his name is Jesus, was raised from the dead. It's hard to believe, but maybe it is true."

"I certainly have been impressed with the love these believers have for one another. They help each other; they make clothing for those who don't have much, and they share food with one another. They are really very kind, loving, and wonderful people. The people in their own Jewish community have turned against them. I know some of them are suffering for lack of income. But that doesn't seem to bother them. They're happy, they're content, and they seem to be very confident of the future. There must be something about their beliefs and teachings that make them live the way they do. I don't know what it is, but it certainly is impressive. If this Jesus can make people be kind and loving and happy, too, there must be something about their beliefs that helps them live with such kindness and confidence."

"Do you think, Gaius, that we ought to try to learn more about this? I don't want to talk about it with Miriam so soon after her husband's death, but I certainly can ask someone in their group about Jesus and his teachings. Jonathan seems to be their leader. Perhaps we should talk with him."

"I think we should, if for no other reason than just to satisfy our curiosity. We're not Jewish, but I really am curious and also very impressed with these people. They may not want us to be part of their group, but—yes, by all means, I think we should talk with Jonathan."

23

—⸎⸎⸎—

JONATHAN

I really don't know what to do. Gaius and Julia have asked a lot of questions about the vision Simon had when he died. They want to know more about Jesus and his teachings. I think they might like to meet with our group of believers. But they're Gentiles. They're not Jews. They're not part of the covenant God made with Abraham. How can we welcome them as believers in Jesus when they do not observe the Torah and Gaius has not been circumcised? Does someone have to be a Jew to become a follower of Jesus, or may we welcome and baptize Gentiles like Gaius and Julia if they confess their faith in Jesus as Lord? I cannot answer that question. I've talked with Daniel and some others in our congregation, and they don't know what we should do either.

I suppose Gaius could go to Rabbi Samuel and be circumcised; they could receive instruction in the Torah. Then as Jews, they could join our group of believers. I can suggest that to them, but I doubt that Gaius would consent to be circumcised, and I don't think he and Julia would want to change their lifestyle to become Jews. I will talk with them again.

The next evening, I go to their home to talk about this issue.

"Gaius and Julia, we have a real dilemma. I know you are interested in learning more about our faith, and we would be happy to have you attend our meetings, but so far, to the best of my knowledge, only Jews have become followers of Jesus. You don't know much about the teachings in our Torah. You haven't been raised to expect the coming of the Messiah. We would like to have you come to our meetings, but I don't know if we are allowed to baptize you and have you become members in our community of faith. The only way I know is for you to become a Jew first. Would you be willing to ask Rabbi Samuel to be circumcised, Gaius?"

"Well Julia and I would like to be a part of your group, but I am not about to be circumcised, Jonathan. I don't see why that is necessary anyway. Didn't Jesus come to help all people? I think I have heard you say that he welcomed Samaritans and Gentiles. He didn't distinguish between Jews and Gentiles in his ministry, did he?"

"You're right, Gaius. Jesus did associate with people who are not Jews. Also, some of our prophets have said that God wants to have all nations and peoples come to him to learn of his ways. But this step is a real departure from the way we have been doing things, and I hesitate to do something that may go against the practices of our faith."

"I can understand the position you are in. I think Julia and I will be satisfied for the present if we may come to your meetings and learn more about Jesus. That will give you more time to find out what groups of followers in other areas are doing. Also by taking some time to learn more about Jesus, Julia and I will become more familiar with his teachings. We are in no hurry to be baptized, but we are really attracted to Jesus and what he has said about God's love. Your God is so much greater and morally better than all the gods in our Roman religions. I can see that God and Jesus are far superior as divine beings to Jupiter, Mars, and Venus. I believe in a God who is powerful and who is more righteous than the ones that are part of our Roman tradition. If Julia and I can attend your group meetings until you find out if we can be baptized, that will satisfy us."

We leave it at that, and I promise I will try to see if there is some way Gaius and Julia and their daughter, Olivia, can be baptized as followers of Jesus. Meanwhile they are starting to come to our meetings every Lord's Day, and we are very happy to have them meet with us. They are anxious to learn all they can about Jesus and his way.

24

—∿∿◦◦◠◟◉◞◠◦◦∿∿—

LUCIUS

It takes over a month for the news of Simon's death to reach me in Antioch. I know immediately that I have to take some time out of my work in the church here to return to Cyrene to be with my family, especially my sister and my two nephews. They certainly must be overwhelmed with grief; Simon meant so much to them. I know the boys are old enough to take care of the farm, and I know my sister well enough to believe she will continue all the work she has to do and will put up a good front for everyone to see. But she must be completely devastated with grief; she loved Simon so much. It was bad enough for her to lose our father; now she has lost her husband as well.

It is not just for Miriam and for Alexander and Rufus that I want to return to Cyrene. I need to go home because of my sorrow too. I feel terrible that Simon suffered such a tragic death. He meant so much to me. He was more than a brother-in-law; he was a wonderful friend. I looked up to him as a mentor and an example of the right way to live. He became almost like a father to me when he married Miriam. What a terrible loss his death is for all of us.

I take a week to wrap up my affairs in Antioch. Then I leave for Seleucia and board a ship heading to Cyprus. We dock at Salamis on the eastern shore of Cyprus to unload some supplies, and then we travel along the southern shore of Cyprus to Paphos, the western port on the island. The ship I boarded in Seleucia is traveling on to Rome, so I disembark in Paphos to wait for a ship that will take me to Cyrene.

Soon I locate a ship that is sailing to Apollonia. I board it to complete my sad journey home.

When I arrive in Cyrene, the entire congregation surrounds me with their love and concern. They comfort me with their good words and sympathy. They also are hungry for information from other groups of believers. I tell them about my work in Antioch and the progress of the church in Jerusalem and Judea. I, in turn, am amazed at the growth of the church in Cyrene, and I compliment Jonathan and Daniel for the leadership they are providing in the congregation.

Jonathan tells me about his dilemma concerning Gaius and Julia. I assure him that Gentiles have been welcomed and baptized as believers in Jesus in other congregations. "In fact," I say, "we have several Gentile believers in our congregation in Antioch." Jonathan is so glad to hear that. Now he can plan a time to baptize Gaius, Julia, and their daughter, Olivia.

After the initial excitement about my return has subsided, I am able to spend time with Miriam and the boys. Boys—I must correct myself, they are now men. They talk about how much they miss their father. But more than that, they really are concerned for their mother. Indeed, as I expected, she is putting up a good front. No one in the congregation or in the community knows how much she is suffering in her grief. Alexander and Rufus say that they hear her crying every night when she goes to her room; she misses Simon so much. She will not talk with them about her grief and even denies that she is crying so much, but they know what they hear.

One afternoon I ask Miriam to go for a walk with me. We head out to the fields where the boys are working. I begin the conversation.

"Miriam, I know how much you miss Simon, and the boys are really concerned for you. They know you are suffering terribly because of your grief."

"I know. I try not to let them know how sorrowful I am. I had a lot of difficulty getting over our father's death, and now I am reliving that and experiencing even greater sorrow because of Simon's death. I try to be strong, and I believe Simon is with Jesus in his Father's kingdom, but I miss him so. I almost wish I could die to be with him again."

"You will be with him again, Miriam, but meanwhile you have things to do here. God needs you and your testimony."

"Yes, I believe that. Did Jonathan tell you that our neighbors, Gaius and Julia, are meeting with us? The good thing that has resulted from Simon's death is that God has led them to our little group of believers."

"You are doing a wonderful thing, Miriam. I'm proud of you. And the community of faith has really grown and prospered here in Cyrene. But that is not what concerns me now. I'm concerned for you, and your sons are too. You have suffered a terrible loss, and it is natural that you are grief stricken. You cannot just shake off that feeling and pretend everything is beautiful. Your sorrow is too real for that."

"Every place I go here in Cyrene I am reminded of Simon. When I walk out here on our farmland, I remember how we used to walk along these paths to work in the fields when we were first married. We couldn't hire help in those days, and we worked side by side planting and reaping. When I am at home, I miss seeing him sitting at our table. When I go out to the market, he is not there with me selling the flour we have milled. And when I go to bed at night, it is almost more than I can endure. He is not there. I can't feel the warmth of his body next to mine. It is at that time that I really cannot bear my sorrow any longer. I admit, I cry and cry long into the night. Then when I get up it starts all over again. I miss him so much, Lucius. He was so kind, such a good and decent man. And he loved me so much. I can hardly bear the loss of my husband."

"Miriam, have you ever thought of leaving Cyrene for a while? You could come with me to Antioch. It would be a change of scene for you and might help you cope with your loss."

"Dear brother, I'm scared of boats and the sea. I don't think I could ever leave Cyrene."

25

—〰◦◖◗◦◖◗◦◖◗◦〰—

MIRIAM

M y brother stays in Cyrene for over two months. He
practically lives at our house as he takes over many of the
chores that Simon had done. He helps the boys manage the
farm. He works in the fields, as Simon did. And he takes care of our
livestock, the couple of horses and goats we have. He takes the stallion
that trampled Simon to his brother's stables. That stallion will go on the
next shipment of horses Joseph takes to Rome. I know Simon's death
was just a terrible accident, but I am happy to see that stallion go.

Lucius and Jonathan meet on many occasions in our home. Lucius
delivers all the news about what is happening in Jerusalem and Antioch
and the growth in the number of believers there. Of course he meets
with our congregation and talks frequently about his experiences. After
Stephen was stoned and the persecution of believers began, many of the
followers of Jesus in Jerusalem scattered to Samaria, Phoenicia, Cyprus,
and Antioch.

One of the most important events that happened was the appearance
of the Risen Christ to Saul, a very promising young rabbinical student
who was studying with the renowned scholar Gamaliel. When Christ
appeared to him in that vision, he was on his way to arrest believers in
Damascus. The vision was so powerful that Paul, the name Saul took
after his conversion, was convinced that Christ was calling him to

become a follower of our Messiah. After his conversion, he went away for several years and then traveled to his hometown of Tarsus.

The leaders of the church in Jerusalem sent a man named Barnabas to Antioch to work with new believers there. Lucius followed Barnabas to Antioch to assist him in strengthening the church there. Around the time Lucius left to come home after Simon's death, Barnabas was traveling to Tarsus to convince Paul to come to Antioch to help with the evangelistic efforts in that important city. Oh, and another thing Lucius tells us is that the followers in Antioch have begun to call themselves Christians, and now that name has spread to believers everywhere. Now we are known as Christians.

The more Lucius says about what is going on in Antioch, the more interested I become in his invitation to go there. I am scared of the sea and of traveling by ships, but still I am interested. When I begin to think about accompanying Lucius on the voyage back to Antioch, I pray earnestly to God to ask him to guide me in this decision. I believe through those prayers that God is calling me to go. Alexander and Rufus are encouraging me to go as well, and I take that as a sign that God wants me to sail to Antioch with Lucius. I am still afraid of the sea, and I have been praying that God will help me to overcome my fear of traveling on a ship so I can go to Antioch.

When Simon died so suddenly and so tragically, I came to realize that the only guarantee in life is that God is with us to encourage, guide, and support us both while we live and when we die. My faith in God is slowly helping me overcome my fear of the sea. I believe I have reached the point where I can go to Antioch with Lucius. Our sons will be able to take care of the farm and our home while I am gone.

When I let people know of my decision to go to Antioch with Lucius, many people stop by our home to wish me well. One of those people is my good friend Joanna. She is the only one of my Jewish friends who has continued to have a relationship with me. She has visited me as often as she could during the past few years. Her husband opposes her having any contact with me, so we have had to be very careful when and where we meet. We have talked a great deal about my faith in Christ. She has said that she would like to become a member of our congregation, but her husband is so opposed to belief in Jesus that he would divorce her if she left the Jewish congregation.

Now, in our last meeting before I am leaving, she says that secretly she does believe in Jesus, and with tears in her eyes, she thanks me for all I have told her about our faith. Even though she loves Matthew, I believe she would leave him to publicly confess her faith in Jesus if it were not for the fact that she would then have no financial support. I will pray for her while I am away.

When my brother and I are ready to leave Cyrene, all the people in our congregation go to Apollonia to see us off. At the dock, Jonathan leads us in prayer for a safe journey to Antioch. I kiss Alexander and Rufus farewell, and Lucius and I board the ship. Moments later, the sailors untie the lines, and we are underway. I feel little pangs of fear, but my faith in God takes over; I know we will have a safe voyage.

It takes us six days to get to Paphos on the island of Cyprus. We have to wait there for several days before we can find a ship to take us to Seleucia. From Seleucia we walk the seventeen miles to Antioch.

When I arrive in Antioch, I am absolutely amazed at the size of the city and at all the activity in it. Lucius and I go to the house where he and Barnabas are living. When we get there, we find that Barnabas has already returned from Tarsus with Paul. Both of these leaders are working to bring in new converts to the faith and to teach them what Jesus said and what we Christians believe. Paul particularly emphasizes the work of the Holy Spirit in his teachings. Paul and Barnabas are so happy to have Lucius return, and they welcome me warmly.

Now I am meeting some of the Christians in Antioch, and when we gather for worship on the Lord's Day, they introduce me to the whole congregation. Everyone surrounds me with their love and comfort and assures me of the salvation we have in Christ. I tell them about Simon's vision as he died, and they praise God that Jesus has welcomed him to his new life in heaven. Their words give me such comfort.

One thing that amazes me about the church at Antioch is that there are many Gentile converts in that congregation. I'm so glad Lucius came to Cyrene to let us know Gentiles are being welcomed into the church. Gaius and Julia, and Olivia too, are now baptized believers, and there certainly will be more Gentiles who will be baptized and join our congregation in Cyrene.

I am learning so much about our Christian faith. As I listen to Paul and Barnabas teach the new converts, my own faith is becoming so much stronger. I still miss Simon and I have my sad moments, but I no longer cry the way I did a month or so ago. I miss my boys and I miss our friends in Cyrene, but I keep busy, and when I listen to Paul and Barnabas teaching the new converts, I become more and more convinced of the truth we have in Jesus our Lord.

My life in the congregation here in Antioch has brought me such great joy! I am so happy God helped me overcome my fear of the sea so I could learn from Paul and Barnabas what it means to follow Jesus.

And I am absolutely amazed at the growth Lucius has experienced here. I cannot call him my little brother any longer. He has become a real inspiration for me.

26

———

LUCIUS

More than a year has passed since Miriam came to Antioch with me. She has been an inspiration to the Christians here. She has witnessed to the people about Simon's life, his carrying the cross for Jesus, and his vision of Jesus when he died. She has assisted in some of the pastoral work we have been doing—meeting with the sick and dying and assuring them of the wonder of God's love and the hope that awaits them in the kingdom of God. But I know she wants to go back to Cyrene. She really misses Alexander and Rufus, and the little bit of news she receives from them does not satisfy her. She wants to return home.

Unfortunately, I do not have time now to return to Cyrene with her, and I don't want her traveling back alone. The Christians in Antioch are about to send Paul and Barnabas on a mission to Cyprus, the island home of Barnabas, and from there to Galatia near Paul's home province in Asia. That means that Simeon, Manaen, and I will be called on to assume more responsibilities as ministers among the Christians in Antioch. I can't leave and expect my co-leaders to handle all the pastoral duties here.

About two months ago, I sent a letter to Alexander and Rufus explaining the situation regarding their mother, and I asked if one of them could come to Antioch to accompany Miriam on her journey home. Just a week ago I finally received their reply. Rufus is on his way and should arrive very soon.

Meanwhile there is a lot of excitement in the congregation here in Antioch. We have become the base for Paul and Barnabas's mission to Cyprus and Galatia. They are making preparations for their journey now. Barnabas has sent word to Jerusalem to ask his young nephew, John Mark, to accompany them on their missionary journey.

In the midst of all these preparations, Rufus arrives in Antioch. He has the opportunity to hear Paul and Barnabas preach and teach the people in the church, and he sees the vitality of the Christian congregations in this city. I know that when he and Miriam return to Cyrene, they will inject some of that same spiritual energy the Holy Spirit has inspired in the congregation here into the company of believers in Cyrene. The Holy Spirit is working miracles before our very eyes.

One Lord's Day when we are worshiping, we feel the power of the Holy Spirit leading us to support Paul, Barnabas, and John Mark to do the work they have been called to do. They kneel before us, and we lay our hands on them to commission them for the very important and difficult mission of taking the Christian faith into cities in Cyprus and Galatia. Rufus and Miriam are present to see the prayer-filled sendoff they receive. The three missionaries set off on the first part of their journey, sailing to Cyprus.

A few days later, I bid farewell to my sister and nephew. They go to Seleucia to board a ship that will take them to Cyprus and then on to Cyrene. I certainly will miss them both. They are so important to me, and Miriam particularly has been such a great help in our ministry here in Antioch. I hope I will see them again before too many years pass.

Cyrene
September, AD 41

27

───〰️◦◖◗◦〰️───

RUFUS

Our return voyage to Cyrene takes longer than we expected. There are strong headwinds that hinder our progress. The sailors are busy day and night tacking back and forth to sail against the winds. I know Mother is worried, but she does not let her fear of the sea overcome her faith in God. She says several times that she is praying very hard that God will bring us home safely. And God does. We finally arrive in Apollonia.

We walk up the hill to Cyrene, and the news quickly spreads that we are back from Antioch. All of our friends in the congregation come to hear about our experiences. Mother tells them about the work Paul and Barnabas have done in Antioch and the wonderful ministry Lucius and his coworkers are doing. I tell them about the commissioning service for Paul and Barnabas and Mark at the beginning of their missionary journey to Cyprus and Galatia. But the most important thing Mother and I relate is the excitement in the congregations in Antioch and the wonderful work the Holy Spirit is accomplishing there. As a result of our report, the congregation in Cyrene begins to pray more earnestly for the inspiration of the Holy Spirit.

Amazing things are happening. First of all, Gaius and Julia are telling their family and friends about Jesus. Several Gentile families are now coming to our worship on the Lord's Day. They are inspired, and soon they will be baptized. The love of Jesus is beginning to pull down the wall of separation between Jews and Gentiles. We are all one faithful community witnessing for Jesus.

We are also praying more earnestly with those who are ill. We go as a congregation, and Jonathan lays hands on the person who is ill; then we all pray for God to heal that person. Many times healing comes quickly. There are some times when the illness persists and a person dies, but we are confident that even in those cases the person's spirit is safe with God.

We are more diligent, too, in reaching out to our neighbors who have need. We take food to women who are widowed, whether they are part of our community of faith or not. Some of the widows in the synagogue are amazed that we are concerned even for them. But they are our neighbors, and even though the Jewish people in the community have turned against us, we still have a Christian responsibility to help them. Every now and then a Jewish family we approach with our help will reject what we bring, but that does not deter us. Jesus said we are to love our neighbors, and just as he taught in the story about the Good Samaritan, our neighbor is any person in need we encounter in life.

Our church is gaining a reputation as a group of people who really love one another and who reach out in love to all the people in the community. The Holy Spirit is blessing us and leading us in our mission to all of our neighbors. God is encouraging us and strengthening us. God is preparing us for the return of his Son to lead us into his kingdom. We believe that day will come very soon. Through the guidance of the Holy Spirit, we are becoming a stronger congregation. People who are not a part of our fellowship are saying, "Look how they love one another."

One of the most important examples of our congregation's compassion involves Mother's good friend Joanna. As soon as we arrived in Cyrene, Joanna came to see Mother. "Miriam," she said, "I feel so strong a call to become a follower of Jesus that I am willing to risk my marriage to Matthew to publically confess my faith and be baptized."

"I know this has been a very difficult decision for you," Mother replied. "When I was in Antioch I talked with Paul about your situation. He said that if one person in a marriage becomes a Christian and the other person does not, they should stay together if the unbelieving person agrees to do so. But if the unbelieving partner does not agree, it is permissible to divorce, and the believer is free to marry another person and not be guilty of adultery."

"I don't believe at my age I will ever marry again. The big problem, however, is that if Matthew divorces me I will have no financial support."

"Let me talk with our elders, Jonathan and Daniel, to see if our congregation will be able to give you the support you need if Matthew divorces you."

Mother talks with Jonathan and Daniel about this. They agree that the congregation will support Joanna with their gifts. When Joanna confesses her faith and is baptized, Matthew divorces her. She loves Matthew and does not want a divorce, but he insists. She moves into our home temporarily, and our congregation makes sure she does not lack for anything. Her daughter and son-in-law stay in touch with her, and eventually they agree to have her live with them.

This divorce creates an even higher barrier between the people in the Jewish congregation and our congregation. I suppose that is the price we pay for our faith in Jesus.

28

─── ∿∾◦◖◗◦◦∿ ───

JONATHAN

As the years go by, our small community of believers grows. One of the most important converts to our faith is Joel, the architect and carpenter who went to Jerusalem with us to celebrate Passover when Jesus was crucified. Daniel is the one who talks with him about Jesus. It all came about in an unusual and providential way. As Rabbi Samuel saw more people in his congregation slipping away to join our fellowship, he began to denigrate Jesus and verbally lash out against faith in our Messiah. In one of his tirades, he said Jesus was just "a no-good carpenter from Galilee." That "no-good carpenter" phrase offended Joel, because that is his profession. A few weeks after Rabbi Samuel made that remark, Joel was working at a home near where Daniel lives.

At the end of the work day, as Joel is leaving, Daniel waves to him. Instead of turning away, as so many people in the Jewish congregation do, Joel motions to Daniel to come out to the road to talk.

Joel begins, "We have been good friends for a long time, Daniel. We haven't seen each other recently, but I really need to talk with you about something Rabbi Samuel keeps bringing up in his sermons. He talks about that no-good carpenter from Nazareth named Jesus who some people claim is the Messiah. I'm a carpenter and it has really begun to bother me that our rabbi keeps mentioning my profession that way.

I know you believe that Jesus is the Messiah and I would like to hear more about him."

"Certainly, Joel, we do believe that Jesus is the Messiah. And we believe because after he was crucified he appeared several times to his disciples and then to a large group of his followers. We believe God raised him from the dead and that through his teachings, his death, and his resurrection he has opened the way for us to enter the kingdom of God."

"Well, I have to hurry home now, Daniel, but maybe we can talk a little more about this some other time."

Several months go by. Then, again in one of those God-given moments, Joel and Daniel cross paths. It is obvious from their conversation that in the weeks between these meetings Joel has thought a lot about faith in Jesus.

"Daniel," Joel addresses his friend, "I am really interested in hearing more about Jesus. Are you willing to come to our home and meet with Hannah and me to tell us more about Jesus?"

"Of course, I am happy to come. Is this evening too soon?'

"No, this evening will be fine. Come after the evening meal."

It takes several meetings with Joel and Hannah before they are ready to make a commitment to follow Jesus and attend our worship services.

They are eager to learn more about following our Lord. Joel and Hannah tell us later that what really attracted them to faith in Jesus was the compassion the members of our congregation show to other people in Cyrene. Our good works are preparing the way for people to come to faith in our Savior.

Once Joel and Hannah are baptized, six of the twelve men who went to Jerusalem to celebrate Passover and their families now are baptized members of our Christian fellowship. Our evangelistic efforts receive a tremendous boost when Joel and Hannah become believers. Joel has contacts through his business with people all over the Pentapolis. Daniel and I work with him to meet people in the other four cities of the Pentapolis and in Apollonia to talk with them about Jesus. Before long we have small congregations of believers in the other four cities in the Pentapolis. One of them, the congregation in Barce, is growing rapidly. The Holy Spirit really is blessing us and our ministry.

But just as we are moving forward in so many wonderful ways, something happens to set back our ministry. One day a visitor from Alexandria arrives in Cyrene. He contacts me, tells me he is a follower of Jesus, and says he has been trained as a teacher in the church in Alexandria. Of course, I welcome him and invite him to our worship on the Lord's Day. He comes and testifies about his faith in Jesus. Then he offers to teach some classes to give us further instruction in the faith. Daniel and I agree and welcome his assistance.

The first several classes go well, and the people in our congregation respond enthusiastically to his teachings. But then he begins to say some things I question. In his instruction he says we really don't have to obey what Jesus taught about being righteous. We don't have to change the way we live because Jesus will always forgive us when we sin.

There are a few people among the recent Gentile converts in our congregation who find this teaching very attractive. They have not been taught about the concept of righteousness from the Law of Moses, and they do not really understand that Jesus came to fulfill the Law. We were praying for them and instructing them on the life they should live as Christians, and they were beginning to see the light. One of them admitted that he was carrying on a promiscuous relationship with his neighbor's wife, and another was being devious in his business relationships. In other ways, too, they were practicing loose and lewd morality. We impressed upon them the high moral standards in Jesus' teachings, and they were beginning to change the way they were living. But now all that progress is lost.

When I recognize the error in this man's teachings and challenge him with Jesus' teachings about righteousness and justice, he becomes very defensive. He is living with one of our families and has received some money from our people for his classes. I order him in no uncertain terms not to teach the people in our congregation any longer and to leave Cyrene immediately. He is not happy with my decision and resists my demands. But when some other men in our fellowship join me in condemning his teachings, he does leave our city.

Unfortunately the families he attracted to his point of view are offended that I ordered him to leave, and they stop coming to our meetings. They apparently decide they can do whatever they wish and that God will forgive and save them. They cannot see how that concept really cheapens the grace of God for which Jesus paid so high a price. It takes several months before our congregation is able to repair the damage from the discord this false teacher has created. Those people who preach cheap and easy grace are a real threat to our faith in Jesus.

29

———∿∿◦ɕⱺᏛᴓᏛᴓᴕᴏ∿∿———

ALEXANDER

I t is now over five years since Mother and Rufus returned from Antioch. I am twenty-five years old, and Mother agrees with me that it is time to consider marriage. We talked about this occasionally over the course of a couple weeks before we really got into a serious discussion of the possibility of my marrying a young woman here in Cyrene. There are some people in our congregation who say no one should consider marriage now because the Lord is going to return very soon. I don't know when Jesus will return to establish his kingdom on earth; people have been saying he is coming back soon for ten years or more, and he hasn't arrived yet. I want to get married, and I am going to take that step and let the Lord return whenever he will.

When Mother and I begin seriously to consider my marrying, I form a very realistic assessment of my situation. "Mother, my choice of a wife is rather limited. I want to marry a Christian woman, and there aren't that many young women available in our congregation here in Cyrene. If I were not a Christian, I would have a wider choice among the Jewish families in Cyrene, but no father in that congregation will consider allowing his daughter to marry a Christian. Rabbi Samuel, too, will never consent to such a union."

"I hadn't really thought about that," replies Mother. "Who is of a marriageable age in our Christian congregation?"

"Well, there are really only two or three I can think of. There is Gaius and Julia's daughter, Olivia. Uncle Caleb's daughter, Leah, is the right age for marriage too, but Jewish Law forbids me from marrying my cousin. Then there is Jonathan's daughter, Suzanna, but she is only about thirteen, a bit too young to be married."

"So the only person who really is available in the congregation for you to marry is Olivia. You have known her since she was born. Do you believe that she would be a good wife for you?"

"Yes, I believe we would be very happy together. But do you think Gaius would consent to have his daughter marry a Jew?"

"I think so," responds Mother. "After all, we are all one in Christ. There is no Jew or Gentile in our congregation."

"Well, who will arrange the marriage since Father isn't here to do it?"

"We'll ask your Uncle Caleb to act in your father's place. He knows Gaius and can make the arrangements for your marriage with him. I'll see Caleb tomorrow and ask him to come to talk with us about this."

The next evening Uncle Caleb comes to our home. He doesn't know why we want to meet, and when he hears our request, he is reluctant to carry out our wishes.

"Alexander, are you sure you should marry a Gentile?" my uncle asks. "You know that is against our Law."

"Well, Uncle, my choices are rather limited. I want to marry a Christian. I can't choose a wife from the families that are still in the synagogue; the fathers of the available women there would never consent to having their daughter marry a Christian, and Rabbi Samuel would absolutely veto any such union."

"Have you thought about marrying Suzanna? If you wait a year or two to be married, she would be of marriageable age."

"Mother and I have talked about that, and we believe that Olivia would be a better choice for me. Will you arrange our marriage with Gaius? You know him well."

"I'll have to think about that. I'm not sure I agree it is a good idea for you to marry a Gentile. I would much rather you put off your marriage for a year or two, and then I can approach Jonathan to arrange a marriage between you and Suzanna."

Had I realized when Mother and I began to talk about my marriage that I would encounter such obstacles along the way, I might have thought differently about proceeding in this matter. It is obvious that Uncle Caleb does not like the idea of my marrying a Gentile. I realize, too, that there are many Jewish Christians in our congregation who feel the same way. The restrictions in Judaism about contacts with Gentiles are to some degree broken down in our Christian faith. We can worship together; we can be part of one Christian fellowship. But to marry is taking this a step beyond where some Jews are willing to go. If this marriage does take place, it will break new ground, and people will have to overcome their prejudices to accept our relationship. I decide I should consult our pastor, Jonathan, and ask him to talk with Uncle Caleb about this matter.

Apparently Jonathan is able to persuade Uncle Caleb that in the Christian community, it is permissible for a Jew and a Gentile, both of whom are Christians, to marry. Uncle Caleb comes back several days later to say he will talk with Gaius to obtain his consent for Olivia and me to be married. I think that now we can move forward to make arrangements for the marriage. How wrong I am!

I am not there when Uncle Caleb and Gaius meet, so I cannot report verbatim what occurs, but as Uncle Caleb tells me later, it did not go well.

For Gaius this marriage proposal strikes at the very heart of the Gentile-Jewish prejudice that has grown so strong in Cyrene. The Gentile majority and the Jewish minority are at odds with one another. The prejudicial actions on both sides of this issue are growing, and Gaius is strongly influenced by the Gentile prejudice against Jews. Even though he is associating with Jewish Christians in our church, he says he cannot approve of his daughter, the apple of his eye, marrying a man who is part of a minority not fully accepted in our city. He turns down Uncle Caleb's proposal. There is no way, he says, he can give permission for his darling daughter Olivia to marry a Jew.

When Jonathan learns what happened, he talks with Gaius about Jesus' acceptance of all people and the fact that we Christians believe God loves all his people and considers Jews and Gentiles to be equals. It is difficult for Gaius to accept this, but after some time passes, he finally agrees reluctantly, I understand, to allow Olivia to marry me. I think Julia may have nudged him in the direction of approving arrangements for our marriage.

Prejudice is a funny thing. It certainly is not logical. It is an emotional response to circumstances that form our understanding of how the social structure in our community should be arranged. It kicks in powerfully whenever we reach a point where it strikes at relationships that are really important to us. And it is very difficult for a person to rise above that emotional response. I can understand why Uncle Caleb and Gaius had so much difficulty getting past the ingrained prejudices that are so evident in our social structure in Cyrene.

When Gaius finally gives his permission for Olivia to marry me, you would expect that we could move forward quickly to the wedding. But again we hit a difficult place. Our wedding is the first in our Christian community to involve a Jew and a Gentile. In fact, our wedding is only the second to be held in our Christian community. In the first both the bride and groom were Jewish Christians, and they followed the custom of being married according to the traditions of Judaism. Jonathan, as our pastor, officiated in that ceremony as a rabbi would in a traditional Jewish ceremony—of course, with the addition of vows that include references to Jesus as our Lord.

In our Jewish community, a marriage begins with a betrothal that is legally binding on both the bride and the groom. During the betrothal period, the two are legally bound to one another even though they are not living together. In the Gentile world there is an engagement, but it is not legally binding. Either party can back out of the arrangement if one or the other chooses to do so. In deference to Gaius and Julia's customs, Olivia and I decide that we will follow the Gentile option. We agree that we will be engaged to be married, and I present her with a ring, which is the custom in the Gentile community. This pleases me because the Jewish betrothal is for a year while the Gentile engagement does not last for any specific period of time.

There is one other detail to be worked out. Among the Jews, the groom pays a dowry to the bride's family to compensate them for the loss of their daughter. Among the Gentiles, the bride's family pays a dowry to the groom to help him set up the household for their daughter.

By this time, Olivia and I have a say in the matter, and we decide under the circumstances we will completely forgo any dowry. Finally, all the arrangements are made, and our two families reach an agreement on the date for our marriage.

On our wedding day, Julia, Olivia's mother, helps her dress and fix her hair. Her dress is a straight tunic with a band of wool tied around her waist. In the Gentile custom, only I am allowed to untie the knot when we are together in our home. Over the wedding tunic Olivia wears a brightly colored veil. At the appointed hour, we meet in the atrium of Gaius and Julia's home. All our friends from the congregation are there, and Jonathan is present to conduct the simple wedding service. We take our vows to be faithful to one another, promising in the name of Jesus our Lord that we will live together in the bond of Christian love.

At the conclusion of the marriage service, Gaius and Julia provide a wedding dinner for us and all of our guests. After this meal, the people escort Olivia and me to our new home, and Olivia goes through the ritual of anointing the door with oil, the symbol of plenty among the Gentiles. Then I carry her over the threshold so she will not trip as she enters our new home; that would be a bad omen for our marriage.

Finally, after all the arduous negotiations and the ceremony and celebrations, Olivia and I are together. Our joyful marriage begins that day with the good wishes of both of our families and the blessing of our congregation and our Lord Jesus Christ.

30

———~~m∘o⊙e⊙⊙⊙∘o~m———

LUCIUS

When Paul and Barnabas come back to Antioch after their journeys across Cyprus and through Galatia, they tell our congregation about the wonderful results they had from their missionary work. In all the cities they visited in Galatia—Antioch of Pisidia, Iconium, Lystra, and Derbe—they established strong Christian congregations.

The joy we all feel because of the success of their mission is soon shattered by a controversy that breaks out in our congregation in Antioch. Some Christians arrive from Jerusalem and begin to teach that all Gentile men in our congregation have to be circumcised before they can be Christians. Further, they say these Gentile families have to observe the Jewish Law with all its dietary restrictions.

Paul, Barnabas, and all of us in Antioch argue that if this practice were established in the church, it would be very difficult for us to reach out to Gentiles with the good news of Christ. In most cases Gentile men would refuse to be circumcised, and their families would not change their lifestyle to observe the restrictions in the Jewish Law concerning what you may or may not eat. We all believe the Holy Spirit is encouraging us to go into all the world—including the Gentile world—with the gospel. If we require male converts to be circumcised, few of them will accept the gospel, and the church will become simply another small sect in Judaism.

The arguments back and forth grow very contentious. The church is in danger of splitting into two factions. Something has to be done to preserve the unity of our Christian fellowship.

Messages go back and forth between Antioch and Jerusalem, and finally James, the brother of Jesus and leader of the church in Jerusalem, decides to convene a meeting of leaders in the congregations around Jerusalem to resolve once and for all the question of whether Gentiles may become Christians without having to submit to circumcision and the Jewish Law.

The apostles and the elders meet in Jerusalem. I am there to listen to the debate. It begins with some of the Pharisees who had converted to Christianity defending the position that all converts to the Christian faith must first conform to the Jewish Law. They declare that in Christian congregations, all males are to be circumcised on the eighth day after their birth. Older boys and men who are Gentile converts to faith in Jesus have to be circumcised when they decide to commit their life to Christ and are baptized. Then Christians must follow the dietary restrictions in the Law and observe all the other regulations of Judaism.

The Pharisees, of course, are trained in the Law and are very strict in their observance of the Law. I have to respect their devotion to our Jewish faith, and I admire the righteous life they live. No one can question their sincerity and their desire to do what is right, but I cannot agree personally that all Christians have to become Jews first.

In stating their case before the apostles and the elders of the church, these Pharisees make a very persuasive presentation. The person representing their point of view says, "We Jews are God's chosen people through the covenant God made with Abraham. Our identity as God's people is confirmed by our observing the Law God gave to Moses on Mt. Sinai. The Law provides us with specific regulations concerning our worship, our behavior, and our life together in our community. The Law stipulates that we are to avoid worshiping idols. The Law says we are to have only one God, not multiple gods like the Gentiles do. The Law lays out certain ethical regulations we Jews must follow. The Law sets us apart from other people by our Sabbath observance and by our dietary laws. And most of all, the Law says we are a peculiar people identified by the sign of the covenant: circumcision. We bear on our bodies the sign of our covenant with God.

"Gentiles, however, are pagans. They worship multiple gods. They eat food they purchase at the temples to their gods, food that has been offered to idols. They have temple prostitutes and practice fornication in their temples. These practices are offensive to all of God's chosen people. If Gentiles wish to become Christians, they have to renounce all of these practices and follow the Law as the chosen people of God.

"Furthermore, Jesus was a Jew, circumcised on the eighth day after his birth, Jesus studied the Jewish Law, and Jesus said he did not come to destroy the Law but to fulfill it. If indeed that is true, then certainly all the followers of Jesus should follow his example. The Law was important to Jesus, and it should be equally important to all of his followers." The Pharisee Christians and others of their persuasion believe their strong and cogent arguments will win the debate.

After the Pharisees speak, the apostle Peter rises to speak. He tells the story of how the Holy Spirit guided him to bring the good news to the Gentiles. He was in Joppa staying with Simon the tanner. At noon on a particular day, he went up on the roof of Simon's home to pray. He fell into a trance and had a vision: "I saw the heavens open, and a large sheet came down. In the sheet were all kinds of animals—four-footed creatures, reptiles, and birds. A voice out of heaven said I should kill and eat. But I protested. I said that I could not eat anything that was unclean. But the voice from heaven responded: 'What God has made clean, you shall not call unclean.' This vision was repeated two more times. To me this was a sign that we are not to be bound by our Jewish dietary laws.

"But what happened next," continues Peter, "changed my view on this issue and convinced me that the good news is for all people, Jews and Gentiles. When I came down from the roof after I had seen that vision, three men appeared at Simon's door asking for me. They said they came from Caesarea and that they had been sent by a Roman centurion named Cornelius. Cornelius had a vision in which he was instructed to send people to find me and invite me to come to his home. Of course, I went.

"The next day Cornelius gathered his family and all of his servants, and when I began to testify to them about the Lord Jesus, the Holy Spirit came upon them, and they decided to follow Jesus. This confirmed for me that God wants us to take the gospel to all people, Jews and Gentiles. We are all saved by the grace of our Lord Jesus.

"Since I had that experience, we have been baptizing Gentiles who believe Jesus is Lord, and we have not required them to be circumcised and follow the Law. We have accepted them as brothers and sisters in faith. There is no distinction between Jew and Gentile in Jesus Christ. Why are some of you placing a restriction on our mission to take the good news to all people?"

When Peter finishes speaking, there is silence in the assembly. Then Barnabas rises to speak. Barnabas became a Christian at Pentecost, and all the people in the church at Jerusalem respect him. Barnabas briefly tells of the journey he and Paul had made to Cyprus and Galatia.

"In every city we visited," says Barnabas, "we went first to the synagogue to teach the people about the coming of the Messiah in Jesus. There were people among the Jews in those cities who believed and were baptized. They formed the nucleus for the community of faith there. But as you know, in every synagogue there are Gentiles who also come to Sabbath worship because they are attracted by the righteous lives we Jews live. These Gentiles were even more open to the gospel of Jesus than the Jews, and when they confessed their faith in Jesus, we baptized them. They became important members of the church in each city we visited. Some of them are now leaders in those congregations. I am convinced the opportunity to serve Christ must be open to Gentiles without any restrictions except that they profess faith in Jesus as their Lord. We should not put any barrier, like a need to be circumcised, before Gentiles who want to become followers of the Lord."

When Barnabas finishes speaking, Paul rises to address the assembly. "I would like to confirm everything my coworker, Barnabas, has said," Paul begins. "The Gentiles are ready to receive the good news about Jesus. They have responded enthusiastically to our preaching. The Holy Spirit has come to them, and many of the Gentile converts are faithfully witnessing to the truth Jesus has given to us. Their witness is bearing fruit in amazing ways. Barnabas and I can cite one story after another to illustrate how God has been working among Gentile converts to bring more people into the church.

"No one can question the fact that I am a Jew and that I have been fully committed to our Jewish faith and traditions. I was circumcised on the eighth day, as our Law prescribes. My parents are Jews of the dispersion, and they were very faithful in observing every aspect of the Law. I am a member of the tribe of Benjamin, well versed in the language and traditions of our people. I was a Pharisee, a student of Gamaliel, and I strictly obeyed the Law. I persecuted the followers of Jesus. I was on the way to Damascus, where I planned to arrest and imprison the Jews who were followers of Jesus, when the risen Christ appeared to me. God had other plans for me. I committed my life to the work of winning converts to Jesus the Messiah.

"Barnabas and I have had amazing success in bringing the good news of Jesus to both Jews and Gentiles in the cities we have visited. Many Gentiles are anxious to receive the good news of salvation through Jesus Christ. If we decide all converts must be circumcised, we will forever be just a small sect among the Jews. Very few Gentiles will join the Way. We have an amazing opportunity to bring our Messiah to the world, as our prophets have instructed. Please do not place heavy restrictions on our mission."

It is obvious that the testimony of Peter, Barnabas, and Paul have carried the day. At this point James rises to speak. "When my father and mother took Jesus to the temple forty days after he was born, a man of God named Simeon declared that now he could depart from life in peace because he had seen in Jesus the salvation that had been prepared by God for all people. He said Jesus would be a light for revelation to the Gentiles and for glory to our people Israel. This confirms what our prophets have said that all people may seek the Lord, even all Gentiles who have called on God's name. So I have made a decision. We shall not trouble these Gentiles with the restrictions of our Jewish Law.

"However, there are several practices among the Gentiles that are offensive to us Jews. We will ask Gentile converts to abstain from purchasing and eating food that people have offered to idols at their pagan temples, to keep from eating meat from animals that have been strangled and still have blood in them, and to refrain from fornication."

When James gives his decision on this matter, the assembly decides they will write a letter that will go to all the congregations in Antioch and in other parts of Syria and Cilicia to communicate the decision they have reached.

I ask if I may carry one of these letters to Cyrene since I know the church there has baptized several Gentile families. The elders give their permission, and I leave Jerusalem for my journey home the next day.

31

—⁓⊶⧫⊷⁓—

JONATHAN

As soon as Lucius arrives in Cyrene, he comes to my home to deliver the letter from the council at Jerusalem. The decision the church leaders have made is good news for us, because we have several Gentile families that have been worshiping with us. Gaius and Julia have invited several of their friends to be part of our fellowship, and Alexander and Olivia have been busy evangelizing some of the younger couples who are their friends. Now that the way is clear for us to expand our fellowship among the Gentiles, we can move aggressively with an evangelistic effort to convert Gentiles in the Pentapolis.

Lucius brings me up to date on the expansion of the church into Cyprus and Galatia. "The pioneer mission work done by Paul and Barnabas in Galatia has brought outstanding results. These two missionaries have established strong congregations in Antioch of Pisidia, Iconium, Lystra, and Derbe. Now they are planning a second journey to visit these four congregations and then to move on to new territory in the Greek world. It is amazing what the Holy Spirit is accomplishing. People really are hungry for good news."

"I know they are, Lucius. I can see that in our congregations here. When we grew to the point where we could not meet in one home, we decided to divide our congregation and meet in two different homes. That worked for a while. Daniel led one of the congregations, and I led the other one. But soon we realized it was important for us to meet and work together as one body in Christ. Isaac has a building on his property that originally he used to store wheat and barley, but then he constructed a new building that more adequately meets his storage needs. The old building was standing idle. We decided to fix it up to use for our worship and teaching ministry. Now Daniel and I share the leadership of the congregation. We also have invited Rufus to study and work with us. Someday, hopefully, we will turn the leadership of the congregation over to him and others we will train."

"Jonathan, you and Daniel are doing a wonderful job here in Cyrene. Every time I return to visit home I see how much growth there has been among those who have committed their lives to Christ. It is very encouraging to me to see how this congregation is growing in faith."

"Thank you, Lucius, your counsel means so much to me and to everyone in our congregation."

On the Lord's Day after Lucius arrives, we gather for worship. Lucius delivers the message.

"Fellow Christians, it is so good for me to return to Cyrene to see all of my friends here. I want to congratulate Jonathan and Daniel for the good work they are doing and thank you for your commitment to Jesus and the faithful service you have given him here in Cyrene.

"We are beginning to reach out into the whole world with the good news of Christ and his victory over sin and death. Paul and Barnabas recently completed a journey to cities in the province of Galatia, where they established strong churches in Iconium, Antioch in Pisidia, Derbe, and Lystra. My sister Miriam was with me in Antioch six years ago when we commissioned them and sent them on their way.

"One of the things that has happened in the church is that Gentiles have begun to respond to the gospel message. You have several Gentile families in your fellowship here in Cyrene, and we rejoice in that.

"Christ told us to go into all the world, and the prophet Isaiah has said we are to be a light to the Gentiles. As a result of the work Peter and Paul and Barnabas have done, Gentiles have become Christians, and some of them have become leaders in our congregations.

"There are some, however, particularly among the Pharisees in Jerusalem, who have said that Gentiles who want to come into the church must follow the Law of Moses. They must be circumcised and follow all the dietary laws we Jews observe. We have now settled this matter that has created great controversy in the church.

"I have just come from a meeting of the leaders of the church in Jerusalem. After both sides of the debate had been presented, James, the brother of Jesus, made a decision—a wise decision, I believe, for the future of the church. The apostles and elders affirmed his decision. They sent a letter to the churches in Antioch, Syria, and Cilicia. I have a copy of the letter, and I would like to read it to you.

"The brothers, both the apostles and the elders, to the believers of Gentile origin in Antioch and Syria and Cilicia, greetings: since we have heard that certain persons who have gone out from us, though with no instructions from us, have said things to disturb you and have unsettled your minds, we have decided unanimously to choose representatives and send them to you, along with our beloved Barnabas and Paul, who have risked their lives for the sake of our Lord Jesus Christ. We have therefore sent Judas and Silas, who themselves will tell you the same things by word of mouth. For it has seemed good to the Holy Spirit and to us to impose on you no further burden than these essentials: that you abstain from meat of animals that have been sacrificed to idols or strangled with the blood still in them, and from fornication. If you keep yourselves from these, you will do well. Farewell.[11]

"There are a few restrictions," continues Lucius, "but our Gentile converts are free from the dietary laws of the Jews and from circumcision. This will make it so much easier for us to talk with Gentiles concerning commitment to our Lord. And it will help you in your mission to all the people in the Pentapolis.

"I am pleased that I am able to bring you these glad tidings, and I pray that God will continue to bless you in your mission to the people in Cyrene and the other cities here. God bless you."

The next morning Daniel and I meet with Lucius to discuss further the work we are doing in Cyrene. We tell him that the work of ministry is growing almost to the point that we cannot keep up with all the responsibilities. Lucius suggests that we organize as some other congregations are doing. We should appoint deacons, men and women, to carry on the work of compassion—taking food to those in need, visiting the sick, and helping to provide blankets and clothing for

people who do not have enough. People in the congregation can n...
the articles that are needed; not all the work of compassion should fal
on the deacons, but the deacons would be in charge of contacting people
on a regular basis to make sure they have all the provisions they need.

He also says some congregations are appointing presbyters—that
is, elders—who conduct the preaching and teaching ministries of the
church. He appoints Daniel and me to be the elders who concentrate on
those duties. When the deacons relieve us of the burden of conducting
the ministry of compassion for the congregation, Daniel and I can focus
on preaching the gospel and teaching our people.

We talk a little about Rufus and the plans we have for him to study
to become another one of the elders in this congregation. Lucius thinks
this is a good idea, and he commends us for the work we are doing in
the church in Cyrene. It really is an inspiration for us to have Lucius
in Cyrene again. He stays for about six weeks before he feels he has to
return to Antioch. We are certainly pleased that such a fine Christian
leader has come from our community.

32

~~~~~~~~~~~~~~~~~~~~~

RUFUS

I have spent several years studying with Jonathan to pursue my work to prepare for ministry in our congregation. For a year or so now, I have begun to notice Jonathan's daughter, Suzanna, when I am in their home. She is a beautiful young woman. I think she has taken some notice of me too.

I am old enough to be married, and Suzanna is as well. First I will talk with Mother, and then I will ask Uncle Caleb to contact Jonathan for his consent to my marrying Suzanna. Arranging our marriage should not be nearly as complicated as arranging Alexander and Olivia's marriage was. There are no impediments I can see if Jonathan agrees to our relationship, and I cannot think of any reason he would not.

When I talk with Mother about my marrying Suzanna, she agrees to contact Uncle Caleb on my behalf. She does so the next day.

Uncle Caleb comes to talk with Mother and me this evening. "I want to assure you that I wholeheartedly approve of Rufus's desire to marry Suzanna and I certainly will talk with Jonathan to see if he and Suzanna are willing to go forward with plans for this marriage. I assume, Rufus, that you are sincere in your desire to marry Suzanna."

"Oh, yes, Uncle Caleb, I certainly am. She is a wonderful young woman and I believe we will be very happy together."

Mother adds, "Rufus and I have talked about his marrying Suzanna and I certainly approve. I am sure if Simon were alive he would give his unqualified consent as well."

"I'm sure he would, Miriam. Rufus, I will talk with Jonathan as soon as I possibly can arrange a meeting. I can see no reason why he would not want you and Suzanna to marry."

The next morning when I go to Jonathan's home for a regularly scheduled session in which he is teaching me about the Old Testament prophecies concerning the coming of the Messiah, Suzanna passes through the courtyard of their home on her way to help her mother. She glances at me and smiles. My heart skips a beat, and I completely lose my focus on the lesson. Jonathan notices I am not paying attention.

"What's wrong, Rufus. I assume you are familiar with this passage we are studying. Are you ill?"

"No, no. I'm not ill. I just can't seem to focus on the lesson. I let my mind wander, I guess."

"Well, that certainly can happen. Do you want to continue?'

"I don't know. Maybe we ought to stop for today. I'm sure I will be able to do a better job with my studies tomorrow."

"All right, let's stop for today. We'll pick up on this lesson tomorrow. I'll see you then."

When I leave, I feel like I am walking on air.

Two days pass. I cannot bear the suspense. Finally, on the third day Uncle Caleb comes with the news that Jonathan and Suzanna have agreed to the marriage. The next Lord's Day, in front of the congregation, Jonathan makes the announcement that Suzanna is going to marry. He doesn't say immediately whom she will marry, so the people in the congregation press him for more details. Then he asks Suzanna and me to come forward, and we are formally betrothed.

In the tradition of the Jewish people, a year passes before we come together as husband and wife. On our wedding day, my family goes to the bride's home, where many people from our congregation crowd into the courtyard for the ceremony. Suzanna and I take our vows before the whole congregation. A very proud Jonathan performs the ceremony.

He almost chokes up when he announces we are husband and wife. Then we enjoy our wedding feast. Following that meal, the people of the church escort us to our home to begin our life together as husband and wife, one flesh united in Jesus Christ our Lord.

33

RUFUS

Suzanna and I have been married now for several years. We have a child who is a year old, a little girl named Naomi, for Suzanna's mother. We have just learned Suzanna is pregnant again. I am hoping we will have a son, but really the only thing that matters is that we have a healthy baby. Both of us are very happy.

But just as we are getting used to the idea that we will have a second child, something very unexpected happens. It seems God enjoys surprising us. John Mark comes to Cyrene. We thought he was traveling with Paul and Barnabas, accompanying them on a second missionary journey to Galatia and the areas beyond that province. But Mark tells us those plans did not work out. On the first journey Paul and Barnabas made to Cyprus and Galatia, Mark traveled with them. He went across Cyprus and into Galatia. He said when they reached Galatia, he had a change of heart and decided to return home to Jerusalem; the journey with Paul and Barnabas was more difficult than he had anticipated. Barnabas, his uncle, understood and accepted his decision, but Paul was very angry that Mark would abandon them at a crucial point in their journey. He considered Mark a deserter in the cause of Christ.

After the council in Jerusalem, Paul and Barnabas made plans to return to visit the churches they had established on their previous missionary journey and then move on to new territory for the gospel. Barnabas wanted to take Mark with them, but Paul absolutely refused.

111

He said Mark was too immature, and he would not take a chance that he might leave them again. Barnabas defended Mark, saying he was older now and more confident and mature, but Paul was adamant. There was no way Mark would accompany them.

For several days, Paul and Barnabas argued back and forth over this issue. Finally, when they could not agree, they decided to go their separate ways. Paul took Silas with him to Galatia and on to the other provinces in Asia and into Greece, while Barnabas and Mark traveled to Cyprus. In Cyprus the two of them labored to strengthen the congregations there. Then Mark moved on, with Barnabas's blessing, to work with the Christians in Alexandria.

After several years there, Mark decided to come to the Pentapolis. Mark had been born in our area and wanted to visit family here. He planned then to go to Rome to visit the church there. The Christians in Rome had just gone through a difficult time. As the center of the empire, Rome attracted many new residents. The church in Rome began when converts, who moved to the capital of the empire because of business they had there, gathered for worship.

Six years ago, there was open conflict in Rome between traditional Jews and Jewish converts to Christianity. The Roman emperor, Claudius, decided he would end the controversy by ordering all Jewish people, both traditional Jews and Jewish Christians, to leave the city. Forced to leave the capital, many of these people went to other urban areas throughout the empire.

Now Claudius is dead. Nero has succeeded him, and the new emperor rescinded the order expelling the Jews. Jews who had been exiled from the capital are beginning to return again to their former homes.

The move of these Jewish Christians back to Rome is creating problems for the church. For six years the congregations in Rome were led by the Gentile Christians who remained in the city. Now Jewish Christians are returning, and some resistance is developing on the part of the Gentile Christians who remained in Rome to allow the returning believers to assume the leadership positions they formerly held.

There are reports that Peter may come from Antioch to Rome to work among the Christians there to resolve some of their current difficulties. Mark is anxious to go to Rome to work with Peter, whom he knew from the time Peter spent in Jerusalem and Antioch.

When Mark talks with Jonathan about his plans, Jonathan says he believes this would be a wonderful opportunity for me to advance my studies. I would have the chance to learn from one who knew Jesus personally and who was a witness of the resurrection, and that is an experience not to be missed. Jonathan is so excited about the opportunity I will have that he persuades Mark to invite Suzanna and me to travel to Rome too.

Now I have to tell my father-in-law that we cannot go to Rome because we are expecting a second baby. Jonathan is delighted with the news that he will have a second grandchild, but he really wants me to have the opportunity to go to Rome to meet the leaders of the church there. In particular, if Peter comes to Rome, a young student like me should leap at the chance to learn about Jesus' ministry from one who spent three years with our Lord. Perhaps I can go alone, he suggests. There is no way I am going to do that. Suzanna and I will be together when our child is born. Then he comes up with another suggestion. My mother can go with us to help us get established in Rome and to help Suzanna care for our second child.

When I talk with Suzanna about this possibility, I am surprised that she is excited about living in Rome. I thought she would want to stay in Cyrene for the birth of our baby, but she is ready to go. Suzanna is an outgoing, adventurous person, willing to do what others might think risky, so we begin to prepare for our voyage. I am thrilled at the many opportunities I will have in Rome, but I am anxious too. I certainly do not want anything to happen that might harm Suzanna or our child. Suzanna brushes off my fears. She says women have been having babies in Rome for many centuries, and she can have a child there as well as in Cyrene. Everything will go well with her pregnancy, she says, and with the birth of our child.

Mother is also enthusiastic about traveling to Rome. For one who was afraid of the sea, she certainly has had a change of heart. It is amazing what faith in God can accomplish.

34

—⁓⦿⊷⦿⊷⦿⊷⦿⁓—

RUFUS

Mark wanted to leave as soon as possible for Rome, so he sailed from Apollonia early in April. Suzanna, Mother, and I have to take care of some matters before we leave Cyrene, so we delay our departure until mid-May. Our voyage across the Mediterranean Sea is largely uneventful. The sea is calm, but because there is so little wind, our voyage takes longer than expected. After five days we catch sight of land, and then it takes another day and a half of sailing up the coast for us to arrive at Ostia, a port city for Rome.

The Tiber River, flowing from Rome to the sea, empties into the Mediterranean at Ostia. Emperor Claudius created a new harbor just north of Ostia, so we sail past the town and the main mouth of the Tiber River to that new harbor. Our captain steers our ship between the lighthouse and the breakwater into the outer harbor and then through a narrow passage into an inner harbor that is hexagonal in shape. Ships from all over the Mediterranean come here to deliver goods for people in the capital. The grain and figs our ship is carrying soon will be off-loaded and put on barges to be drawn up the Tiber River for sale in the markets in Rome. It takes many provisions to supply the needs of the million people who reside in the capital, so this port is indeed a very busy place.

As soon as the lines from our ship are secured and the gangway is in place, we disembark. We are glad to be on *terra firma* again after spending almost a week at sea. We say a little prayer of thanks to God for our safe passage, and then we begin to walk the mile or so from the port to Ostia. It is too late in the afternoon to walk from Ostia to Rome. Mark sent word to us through our ship's captain that there are several Christian families in Ostia who will put us up for the night. Following his directions, we locate the home of Philip, his wife, and his children. They welcome us warmly, serve us a wonderful meal, and provide a place for us to spend the night. We enjoy a delightful time in their home, and we thank God for leading us to such a wonderful host family.

As the sun rises the next morning, we leave Ostia to walk the eighteen miles to Rome. Philip gives us bread to sustain us on our journey. I carry the provisions we have brought from Cyrene while Mother and Suzanna take turns carrying little Naomi. It takes all day for us to arrive at the capital. We have never seen such a large city and so many people. Life in Rome, we quickly realize, will be quite different from life in Cyrene. We cross the Tiber River and enter the city proper. Mark told us how to get from the bridge we cross to the home where one of the Christian congregations in the city meets. There we are warmly welcomed by our new Christian friends, Andronicus and Junia. We will stay in their home until we can find a place of our own. After sharing a meal with our host and hostess and spending an hour or so in conversation and in prayer, we weary travelers retire for the night. Mercifully, Naomi does not wake up before the first light in the morning.

There are two things I need to do as quickly as possible, and I am not sure which is more important. I need to find a place for us to live, and I must find a job to support our family. Andronicus and Junia assure us that we can take our time finding a place to live, but we are anxious to get settled in our own home.

City living is much different from what we experienced in Cyrene. In Rome most people live in apartment buildings, blocks of four or so structures that are connected by common walls and are two or three stories tall. Fortunately I am able to find a first-floor apartment that is within our means. We have brought enough money with us from Cyrene to cover the first three or four months of rent.

Our apartment is not large, only four rooms, but it will satisfy our needs. The only drawback is that it is adjacent to the *Subura,* a district in Rome that is located just east of the Forum. The Subura is where the poorest people in Rome live. Prostitution and crime are rampant there, and the criminal elements have complete control of some of the streets. We realize this is not the most desirable place for us to live, but our apartment is far enough away from the worst areas that we feel relatively safe.

I have the good fortune, because of circumstances in Rome at this time, to receive an offer for an excellent position. Because the emperor now is allowing Jewish families to return to Rome, many former residents are coming back to the capital to live. The Christian families need a teacher for their children. God gave me a good mind, and Jonathan has instructed me not only in the Torah and the prophets but also in mathematics, astronomy, science, philosophy, and literature, so I am well equipped to teach children. When Andronicus and Junia learn of my academic background, they ask me to teach the children of the families in the congregation that meet in their home and any other children who might be interested in joining them. I gladly agree to take this position, and I am now teaching children who are from six to twelve years old. God truly does provide what we need when we trust him. We are settling into life in Rome.

35

——〜∘ᵔᵕᵔ∘〜——

MIRIAM

R ufus and Suzanna have adapted quickly to their new life in Rome. I have not. In Cyrene we had a home that included a large atrium and an open courtyard. We had a kitchen and a table where we could gather to eat. There were two separate rooms for sleeping and an area for storage. Here in Rome, our apartment is small. We have one room for cooking and eating and three other rooms. Rufus and Suzanna sleep in one of them. Naomi has another one; she and the new baby will share that room. I have the third one for my use.

In Cyrene I also had work to do. I would go to the market to sell flour and bread. Here in Rome, women are not employed. Suzanna and I are expected to stay home. The only activity I have is to go to the market and purchase food for our family. Helping Suzanna care for Naomi provides some diversion from my boredom, but I wish I had more to keep me busy.

Our congregation here in Rome is smaller than the congregation in Cyrene. There are a number of small congregations scattered in different areas of the capital. The believers meet in the homes of the congregations' leaders. Our congregation meets in Andronicus and Junia's home. The women in the congregation gather each morning for prayer and devotions, and that does give me something to do, but there is so much more I believe I could be doing. As Suzanna advances with her pregnancy, I am sure I will need to take more responsibility caring for Naomi, and when the new baby arrives, my work will increase. I know it is important for me to be in Rome with Rufus and Suzanna, but I do miss my life in Cyrene.

There is a certain pattern to life here in Rome. The day begins at sunrise. We eat a small loaf of bread, and then Rufus leaves for his work. In Rome men work for six hours until midday. Rufus works a little longer; the school day goes into the early afternoon, with a small break for lunch. Then in the mid-afternoon, we have the main meal of our day. Those of us who are not so affluent usually have chicken and vegetables for that meal. Our vegetables include broad beans, lentils and chickpeas, lettuce, cabbages, and leeks. On occasion we will add fruits and nuts—apples, pears, wild cherries, plums, grapes, walnuts, and almonds.

People who are well-off have more variety in their meals. They also have slaves who serve them day and night. Some people say that of the million people who live in Rome, four hundred thousand are slaves. I have no way of proving that, but there are many, many slaves in the city. Some worship with our congregation.

Of course, we Christians meet every Lord's Day. Our meeting for worship is similar to what we experienced in Cyrene. When we gather in the afternoon, each family brings food to eat. Andronicus begins our meal with prayer, and we sing a song of praise. Then Andronicus breaks a loaf of bread, inviting all of us to receive this bread that represents the body of Christ. Then we share what we have brought to eat. Following the meal, we receive instruction from Andronicus or Junia concerning our faith. At the close of our time together, Andronicus pours a cup of wine, saying this is the blood of Christ that was shed for us. Then we pass the cup, and each of us takes a sip of that wine. Following a closing prayer, a song, and a blessing, we depart for our homes.

There is a strong sense of fellowship in our congregation, and that creates encouragement and support for our people to be faithful believers. We are very fortunate to have Andronicus and Junia as our leaders. They are truly committed to the Lord.

36

———∿∽◦◦⟨⟨◦⟨◦⟨◦⟩◦◦∿———

SUZANNA

Just a week ago in the evening, my water broke and my labor began. Rufus and Mother Miriam were with me. Junia said she would like to be present to help me with the birth of our second child, so Rufus went immediately to tell her she should come to our home. My labor was relatively brief, and just five hours later our second child was born. It is another girl. I know Rufus was hoping for a son, but he is very excited Naomi will now have a sister to grow up with. I think he remembers how close he and Alexander were in the years they were growing up. We named our new little girl Mary. We considered Miriam, but Rufus's mother said it might be less complicated for people if we chose another name. Mary is as close to Miriam as we could come.

Naomi was so easy to care for when she was a baby. She was a happy baby and cried very little. Mary is quite the opposite. Oh, she is happy, but she cries a lot. It seems that as soon as she gets a little hungry, she lets out a whoop, and I have to get her immediately to nurse her. Sometimes she wants to be fed every two hours, and she has gotten me up twice a night since she was born. I am a tired but very happy mother. Fortunately, Mother Miriam is with us. She takes Mary when I have finished nursing her and walks around, patting her until she goes back to sleep. Mother Miriam and Rufus are almost as tired as I am because every time Mary cries, they wake up too. I think Rufus is glad he can leave each morning to go to teach his classes.

Naomi is just over two years old. She likes her little sister, but I think she is a bit jealous. For two years she has been the center of attention in our family, and now another person who requires so much care has appeared on the scene. We try to give Naomi as much attention as we can, but Mary demands so much of our time. There are a couple other two-year-olds in our congregation and Naomi gets together to play with them, but she still spends a lot of time with me and Rufus. Mother Miriam has started taking Naomi with her when she goes to the market to buy our food. And Rufus has begun to play with her when he returns from teaching in the afternoon. She really enjoys her father's attention.

Our life in Rome has settled into a routine. As soon as it is light, we arise to begin the day's activities. For several centuries the Roman government has given free of charge a daily allotment of grain to families in the city. Rufus dresses and goes three blocks down the street to get our allotment of grain for that day. When he returns, we all have our first meal of the day, which usually consists of a small loaf of bread. Then Rufus leaves to go to teach his students.

Mother Miriam grinds the grain we have received to make bread for the next day, and then she and Naomi go off to the market to shop for the other food we need that day. We usually eat a snack around the middle of the day, and then when Rufus returns in the middle of the afternoon, we have the main meal of the day. Then we spend time together as a family until we put the children to bed and retire for the night. Mother Miriam keeps us firmly on that schedule. It is such a blessing to have her with us in Rome, and I thank God daily for what she does. I know Rufus really appreciates her help too.

Our life in Rome is going well. Rufus loves to teach. Our church family has embraced us, but we still miss our family and church friends in Cyrene. In a few months Uncle Joseph, Mother Miriam's brother, will be coming to Rome with some horses to deliver to the soldiers here. We look forward to the time he will be with us so we can catch up on news from home. God is good and we thank him daily for all of his blessings, even for little Mary's demanding nature. We are sure she will grow up to make her mark in the world.

37

—⁓⚬⚬⚬⚬⚬⚬⁓—

ANDRONICUS

Junia and I have names that sound Roman, but actually we are Jewish. Well, I should correct that. We never really practiced the Jewish faith in my home. My mother was Jewish, and that by definition makes me a Jew. My father was a low-ranking Roman official in Galilee. He was the one who insisted I have a Roman name. He died when I was just a boy. My mother and I stayed in Galilee because that is where her family is.

Junia's family was a bit more religious than was mine, but they were not faithful Jews. They usually observed Passover, and they went to synagogue on occasion, but they never really were committed to the Jewish faith. When we got married, Junia and I decided we would not observe the rituals of our faith.

Junia's sister married a faithful Jew. They attended the synagogue in Capernaum, and one Sabbath a young rabbi named Jesus came there to teach. They began to go to various towns in Galilee to hear him preach, and they would tell us about his teachings and the healings he performed. What they said fell on deaf ears until one day they told us their friend Jesus had been crucified in Jerusalem but that he had appeared to some of his followers after his death. He told his followers they should come to Galilee, where he would meet them before he ascended into heaven. Junia's sister and her husband convinced us we should go with them to the place where his people would meet. We did.

There on that hillside in Galilee we saw the risen Christ; we heard his last charge to his disciples, and we watched as he ascended into heaven. We could not deny what we saw. We immediately became believers. Junia's sister and her husband did too.

In the beginning, the followers of Jesus centered their activities in Jerusalem. We lived in Capernaum, and there weren't that many believers there in the days right after the resurrection. But when the persecution of Jesus' followers began in Jerusalem, believers scattered from the capital city to Samaria, Galilee, and beyond. As more and more followers of the Way came to our area, we began to meet regularly on the Lord's Day for our common meal and worship. It was during those days that Junia and I became very active among the followers of our Lord.

We were still living in Capernaum when Paul was converted. We met him soon after his conversion when he traveled from Jerusalem to his home in Tarsus. Later we met Barnabas; in fact, he spent the night in our home when the church leaders in Jerusalem sent him to Antioch to work with the faithful in that city.

I am a merchant who deals in cloth goods, and Junia and I decided we would move to Rome, where I could expand my business. I became well-to-do here. God really has blessed me. Junia and I were able to acquire a nice home in Rome. We began to invite Christian friends to come to our home for worship on the Lord's Day, and soon our home became one of several in the city where Christians regularly gather to worship. But when Claudius ordered all Jews to leave Rome, Junia and I left with all of our Jewish friends. Fortunately, good friends of ours, a Gentile family in our congregation, were able to care for our home so it would continue to be a center for our congregation's activities. Junia and I were certain one day we would be able to return to our home here.

During the five years of our exile from Rome, we lived in Thessalonica, where I continued my business activities. One day Paul and Silas arrived in Thessalonica; they were coming from Philippi, where they had been imprisoned.

In Philippi, Paul had converted a woman named Lydia, who became a leader in the church there. But trouble for Paul developed in that city. A woman who was a psychic began to follow Paul when he walked along the streets in Philippi. She identified Paul and Silas repeatedly as "slaves of the Most High God." Finally Paul got tired of her interruptions wherever he traveled, and he ordered the spirit of divination to come out of her. It did. Those who managed her affairs now had lost their means of income. They seized Paul and Silas, said they were Jews, and accused them of doing what was unlawful. The officials arrested Paul and Silas, beat them, and imprisoned them.

In the middle of the night, there was an earthquake that knocked open the doors of the prison. None of the prisoners tried to escape. The jailer thought they had all fled, and he was about to commit suicide when Paul cried out to assure him that all the prisoners were still in the prison. The jailer was so amazed that he became a believer on the spot. Paul baptized him, his family, and all of his servants. When Paul and Silas were freed, the people in Philippi thought it best that they leave their city as quickly as possible. Lydia, the jailer and his family, and the others Paul and Silas converted to Christ stayed in Philippi, and the church there grew to be a strong, vital congregation.

Paul and Silas came to Thessalonica after they left Philippi. They went to the synagogue and began to teach people about Jesus. Some of the Jews and a large number of Gentiles were converted. Junia and I were glad to become a part of that growing church.

Unfortunately the Jews in Thessalonica were jealous of Paul's success in converting people to believe in Jesus, and they created an uproar in the city. They tried to apprehend Paul and Silas but could not find them, so they seized several of us and put us in prison until our friends could raise bail to free us. We realized it was too dangerous for Paul and Silas to stay in Thessalonica, so we sent them on their way to Beroea.

Junia and I stayed in Thessalonica until Claudius died and Nero became emperor. Then we were able to return to Rome. We are very happy to be back.

As we Jewish Christians came back to Rome, the Gentile Christians were reluctant to give us the leadership roles we had before. This has created tension between Jews and Gentiles in our congregations in Rome. The Christian fellowship in the congregations that existed before Claudius's edict is severely threatened. The Gentile Christians who meet in our home were willing to welcome us back, but I could tell they harbored some resentment. Fortunately we were able to smooth out these differences so we can again share leadership in our congregation.

Rufus and Suzanna arrived in Rome with their daughter and Rufus's mother soon after Junia and I returned. I immediately recognized that Rufus is very intelligent and an excellent teacher. I recruited him to teach the children in our congregation. I now see his talent and commitment, and I plan to have him take some responsibility in assisting Junia and me in the pastoral work in our congregation. Rufus will be a big help in the months ahead as our congregation grows. We praise God for that!

38

———〰〰᎐᎐᎐᎐〰〰———

MIRIAM

I know it is around this time of year that my older brother, Joseph, usually crosses the Mediterranean with a shipment of horses for the military in Rome, so it is not a complete a surprise when he arrives at our door. How happy we are to see him!

After he arrived at Ostia, he got the dozen horses he was delivering off the ship and into the hands of the man at the dock, who will take them to the soldiers in Rome. When he had been paid for the horses, he set off for Rome to visit us.

What a joy it is to see him again! After we eat our meal, we talk for hours, catching up on all the news. I want to know everything that is happening in Cyrene, and I draw from him every bit of news I can about all the people at home. Naomi does not remember her great-uncle and is a bit shy at first. But soon she realizes he is her friend and she climbs up on his lap. I am delighted to be with my older brother again. Rufus is anxious to know everything that is happening in the church in Cyrene, and Suzanna wants to know how her father and mother are doing. Little Mary really is very good all evening. When Joseph holds her and rocks her in his arms, she coos and makes all the happy noises a baby can.

The next morning Joseph goes with Rufus to his school and sits in on some of his classes. He comments on what a great job Rufus is doing teaching the children in the congregation. He meets Junia and

Andronicus and sees what wonderful people they are. They invite him to stay in Rome for a few extra days so he can come to worship with our congregation. He assures them he has no immediate plans and he will attend worship before he departs for home.

On the next Lord's Day, we all walk to Junia and Andronicus's home. In worship that day, Andronicus asks Joseph to speak about what is happening in the church in Cyrene. Then we all talk about the challenges for us Christians, wherever we may be. In Cyrene there is the tension between the Christian congregation and the Jewish congregation. In Rome there is the pressure to worship the Roman gods. It takes real commitment to be a Christian, whether you are in Cyrene, Rome, or any other place in the empire. That commitment can only be strengthened when we meet together in the fellowship of the Lord.

Joseph stays in Rome for a few more days, but by the middle of the week, he has to start back to Cyrene. We hug, and I shed some tears as my wonderful brother leaves our apartment to return to Ostia to board a ship for his voyage back to Cyrene. I am beginning to feel homesick for the family and friends I left behind when I came to Rome.

39

———ww·◦◦◦◦◦◦◦ww———

RUFUS

Andronicus and Junia are giving me some added responsibilities in our congregation. In addition to teaching the children, I will be assisting them as a worship leader and elder. I really appreciate the confidence they are placing in me. Mother and Suzanna are important people in our fellowship as well. Mother has shared with the congregation what Father experienced when he carried Jesus' cross, and Suzanna has been telling stories about Jesus to Naomi and the other small children in our fellowship.

The exciting news for our congregation is that Peter, the disciple and apostle, is in Rome. He and his young friend Mark are visiting the various congregations in the city. This Lord's Day they will meet with our congregation. What an opportunity it will be to hear what Peter has to say about the days he spent with Jesus! But the greater opportunity is mine. Mark has arranged for me to have a private meeting with Peter today. He knows one of the reasons I came to Rome was to meet Peter and hear the stories he can tell me about the three years he spent in the company of our Savior. When Mark and Peter arrive at our apartment, Mother, Suzanna, and the girls go to the market, giving me the opportunity to have a private conversation with this disciple and church leader.

After some introductory conversation, I begin to question this remarkable church leader. "What was Jesus really like?" I ask. "My father said he had such a kind expression even when he was walking to his death, and that he had the quiet confidence that God was with him. You had so many different experiences with him. Tell me your impression of him."

"Jesus was a kind and compassionate man. He also was a man of great strength and conviction. When he first invited Andrew and me to follow him, he was so open and welcoming that we did not hesitate one moment to give up our work as fishermen to be his disciples. He was a healer, and one of the first times I was with him, he healed my wife's mother. I think in the beginning of his ministry in Galilee, it was his healing miracles that brought crowds of people to hear him. The people loved him and recognized that he taught with great conviction. He knew what God wanted him to say and do. His mission was clear."

"What is the key to that great faith he showed in his ministry?"

"He spent time alone with God. He would steal off early in the morning to pray to his Father in heaven. At first we disciples couldn't figure out why it was so important that he carry out this discipline, but soon we realized that this time alone with God was necessary for him to understand what his Father in heaven wanted him to do. He nurtured that relationship with God, and because he did, he knew God was with him, helping him to preach and teach to fulfill his mission in the world. I never saw him waver from the good work God gave him to do."

"If you were to sum up his teachings in a short and simple way, what would it be?"

"You know, in the years since I was with Jesus, I have thought a lot about that question. Of course, he centered his whole life and his teachings on the summation of the commandments, that we are to love God with all of our heart, soul, strength, and mind and love our neighbors as ourselves. But beyond that I would say that the key to understanding his teachings is to be found in the word *humility*. We are to be humble.

"Jesus was really hard on the Pharisees. He called them white sepulchers, clean on the outside but filthy within. He didn't hate these men; he loved them. But the flaw he saw in them was that they were so very proud of their own righteousness. Because of their pride in the good things they do, they seem not to need God. They fulfill the commandments; they do what they believe God wants them to do. In their minds, they have satisfied all the requirements for God's approval. They don't understand that spiritual pride is their sin. They do not see that they need to develop a relationship with God in which they trust God to be their guide and help.

"You know, Jesus was a great teacher, using stories to make his point. In one story he told, two men went up to the temple to pray. One was a Pharisee, a very righteous person, and the other was a tax collector, a sinner hated and reviled by the people. The Pharisee prayed, 'God, I thank you that I am not like other people: thieves, rogues, adulterers, or even like this tax collector. I fast twice a week; I give a tenth of my income.' Meanwhile the tax collector prayed, 'God be merciful to me, a sinner.' Jesus said to us disciples, 'I tell you the tax collector went home justified in God's eyes, for all who exult themselves will be humbled and those who are humble will be exalted.' The Pharisee thought he didn't need God. He believed he had satisfied all the requirements God has for believers. The tax collector knew he needed God's help. I often recall that story because there are so many times when I let my pride get in the way of my relationship with God. You have to be humble to realize how much you need God's help."

Mark interjects, "What I see in this story that Jesus told is that pride not only harms our relationship with God but with other people as well. The Pharisee obviously thought he was better than everyone else, certainly better than that tax collector. That pride created a barrier between him and the tax collector. He would not have anything to do with such a lowly sinner as that man."

"And," Peter continues, "there was that time when we disciples realized Jesus was in danger of being seized. We believed he would then overthrow the power of Rome and establish his kingdom on earth. James and John, two brothers among the disciples, went to Jesus privately and asked that when he established his kingdom, he would let them be on his right and left hands, sharing authority with him.

"When I heard what had happened, I was angry. So were the other disciples. I was the most prominent of the disciples, the leader, and I figured that I should have that kind of authority in Jesus' kingdom. When Jesus saw that we were so angry, he called us together and in a very kind and gentle voice said, 'Whoever wants to become great among you must be your servant, and whoever wishes to be first must be the slave of all; I didn't come to be served but to serve, and to give my life for all people.' We didn't realize what he really was saying at that moment; we found out later when he gave his life for all of us."

"So humility, then, is the one word that sums up all the teachings of Jesus," I say.

"Yes. Be humble before God; recognize you are a sinner who needs God's forgiveness, guidance, and strength, and be humble in your relationships with other people. Don't think of yourself more highly that you ought. You have certain gifts and abilities, but you are no better than other people. It is only when you are humble that you can love God with all your heart, soul, strength, and mind, and it is only when you are humble that you are able to love and serve your neighbor."

"What are some other teachings of Jesus that you think are important for us to hear so we may be more like him?"

"Well, one thing Jesus often criticized is making a show of how religious you are. Jesus thought your faithfulness should be apparent in the way you live. He didn't approve of people showing off how good they think they are. I remember a time when we were in the temple in Jerusalem, and a wealthy man came in to display how great his religious commitment was. He took a bag of coins and dumped them in the box for offerings in the temple. When the coins hit that metal container, they made a lot of noise, and everyone looked around to see who was being so generous. The man obviously took great pride in the attention people paid to his generosity. Then a very poor woman, a widow, came to the same container and put in two little coins. No one paid any attention to her—no one except Jesus. He said to us that this poor woman had given more than all the other people, for they gave from their abundance while she gave everything she had. The man made a big show of how religious he was, but the woman was the one who showed her true commitment."

"You mentioned before that you disciples thought Jesus would bring in his kingdom when he was seized by the authorities, but it didn't happen as you expected. When do you think his kingdom will come?"

"I wish I could give a good answer to that question. We expect it to happen any time, but we have been waiting for over twenty-five years. We thought it would come before those of us who were living when Jesus was on earth died. But many of us have already died, and I am beginning to wonder if it will happen before I die. I think now that it is time for us to write down some of the things Jesus said so people will remember his life and teachings. I've been talking with Mark about doing just that. There are church leaders in Jerusalem who are compiling and distributing in written form a collection of Jesus' teachings. If Jesus were to come tomorrow, it would not be necessary to write about him, but if he doesn't come for a generation or two or even longer, it will be important to record what he said and tell the story of what he did. I'm depending on Mark to remember all the stories I am telling him so he can write a story of Jesus' life, death, and resurrection."

"You mentioned Jesus' resurrection. Tell me, what was it like to see him alive after he had died on the cross?"

"That was the most amazing thing. When Jesus was arrested, we disciples ran and hid. We were afraid. I hung around a little bit, and a couple of people said I had been with Jesus. I lied. I denied I had ever known him. When we disciples got together after Jesus died, we figured it was over; we might as well go back to what we were doing before we had met Jesus. I was ready to go back to Galilee to begin fishing again. Then the next day, some women who planned to prepare Jesus' body for burial reported that the tomb was empty.

"I ran out to see for myself, and they were right; his body wasn't there. That evening we all gathered in the Upper Room where we had observed the Passover. We locked the door because we were afraid the authorities might come for us too. While we were there, Jesus appeared to us. He made appearances several other times as well. We were convinced God had raised him from the dead. Then we waited, and on Pentecost the Holy Spirit inspired us to go to declare the good news that Jesus is the Messiah. After that there was no turning back, and today there are faithful communities of Christians all around the Mediterranean Sea. We truly have gone into all the world as he has commanded us."

"I certainly cannot add anything to what Peter has told you," Mark comments, "but I can say that when people gathered after their conversion at Pentecost, they wanted to learn all they could about what Jesus did. Lucius, Jonathan, and Daniel were part of that group. It was the resurrection that convinced us who knew Jesus, as my mother and I did, that he is the Messiah and we should follow him. The resurrection opened our eyes so we could see that Jesus in not just a rabbi or a healer. He is our Lord and Savior."

At that point in our conversation, Mother, Suzanna, and the girls return from the market, and our conversation changes. Peter asks Mother to tell him about the experience Father had at the crucifixion of Jesus. She goes into great detail, and both Peter and Mark are grateful to have Father's memories of the crucifixion.

Soon our two guests say they have to be on their way, and they will see us the next Lord's Day when our congregation meets. We bid one another a grateful shalom. I am so happy to gain more insight into the life and teachings of our Lord from one who knew him so well.

40

—◦◦◦◦◦◦◦◦◦—

ANDRONICUS

On this Lord's Day all the people in our congregation gather in Junia's and my home for worship. It is a special day; everyone is excited because Peter is meeting with us. We begin as we normally do—by singing a hymn and having a prayer. The hymn we sing is one recently given to us by a leader in another congregation. It is a wonderful hymn that says we should have the mind of Christ, putting away pride and being humble before God and all people. Everyone in our congregation has committed the hymn to memory.

> Jesus Christ, though he was in the form of God did not regard equality with God as something to be exploited, but he emptied himself, taking the form of a slave, being born in human likeness, and being found in human form, he humbled himself and became obedient to the point of death—even death on a cross. Therefore God also highly exalted him and gave him the name that is above every name so that at the name of Jesus every knee should bend, in heaven and on earth and under the earth, and every tongue should confess that Jesus Christ is Lord, to the glory of God the Father.[12]

After the hymn, we share the food people have brought. Then Peter rises to speak.

"Fellow Christians, I am so happy to be with you this Lord's Day to share in your fellowship and to have the opportunity to speak to you about some of the experiences I had with Jesus when we walked along the dusty roads of Galilee. This afternoon I want to tell you about three special experiences I had with our Lord.

"We disciples were walking with Jesus between two villages in the district of Caesarea Philippi when we stopped to rest. We gathered around Jesus. He asked us, 'Who do people say that I am?' We all gave the answers we had heard from people who gathered to hear him teach: 'Some say you are John the Baptist who has returned, others say Elijah or one of the other prophets.' 'But who do you say that I am?' asked Jesus. I immediately blurted out, 'You are the Messiah.' Jesus commended me. He called me 'the Rock,' and then he told us not to tell anyone he is the Messiah. He began then to tell us that he would be going to Jerusalem, where he would endure great suffering and would die, but that in three days he would arise from the dead. I blurted out that this could not be; the Messiah will not suffer and die. But Jesus rebuked me, saying I was Satan for uttering such a thing. I went from being the Rock to being Satan in just a few moments. I was hurt and perplexed, but that was not the last time I would feel that way.

"A few days later, Jesus asked James and John and me to go up on a mountain with him. We were happy for the chance to be alone with him. When we got to the top of the mountain, Jesus suddenly changed right before our eyes! His clothing became dazzling white, and there was an aura all around him. Then Moses and Elijah appeared, and they spoke with Jesus. We three disciples did not know what to say, and I uttered one of those stupid things I am so famous for: 'Let's make three dwellings here on the mountain, one for you, one for Moses, and one for Elijah.' Jesus just looked at me as if I didn't know what I was saying. Then a voice came out of heaven, saying, 'This is my Son, the Beloved, listen to him.' At that point the vision ended, and only Jesus and we three disciples were there. We started back down the mountain. Once again I couldn't figure out what all this meant.

"The third incident was very painful for me. After we all met in the Upper Room to celebrate the Passover, we went out to the garden of Gethsemane, and Jesus said soon he would be seized and all of us disciples would desert him. Again I was the first to speak: 'Even though all become deserters, I will never leave you.' Jesus said, 'Tonight before the cock crows you will deny me three times.' I vehemently declared I would not, but I am ashamed to say that is exactly what I did. Three times I denied that I had ever known him.

"I didn't understand what was happening. I failed to recognize my own weakness and fear; I thought I was strong when I was not. All through those times when I said I didn't know him, I simply could not believe the Messiah had to suffer and die and then be raised again to new life. The wonderful thing for me is that I now know Jesus has forgiven me. It's amazing that after my denials, the Risen Christ has accepted me again."

At this point Peter offers the prayer our congregations uses before we break the bread for our sacred meal.

> We thank you, our Father, for the life and knowledge you made known to us through Jesus your Servant; to you be the glory forever. Even as this broken bread was scattered over the hills, and we gathered together the wheat and flour to make one loaf, so let your church be gathered together from the ends of the earth into your kingdom, for to you is the glory and the power through Jesus Christ forever. Amen.[13]

Then Peter breaks the loaf of bread representing the broken body of our Lord, and we pass it so all who have gathered can receive this food for our spirits. Then Peter takes the cup that is before him and says,

> We thank you, our Father, for the holy vine of David your servant that you made known to us through Jesus your Servant; to you be all glory forever. And now may we receive this cup filled with the wine that is the blood of Christ that has been shed for the forgiveness of my sins and of your sins. Let us all drink from this cup.[14]

We pass the cup, and all of us take a sip of wine from it. Then Peter offers the closing blessing.

> We thank you, Father, for your holy name, which you have caused to dwell in our hearts, and for the knowledge and faith and immortality you made known to us through Jesus your Servant; to you be the glory forever. You, Master almighty, have created all things for your name's sake. You gave food and drink to people for enjoyment, that they might give thanks to you, but to us you have freely given spiritual food and drink and life eternal through your Servant. Before all things we thank you that you are mighty; to you be the glory forever. Remember, Lord, your church, to deliver it from all evil and to make it perfect in your love, and gather it from the four winds, sanctified for your kingdom, which you have prepared for it, for yours is the power and the glory forever. Let grace come, and let this world pass away. Hosanna to God, hosanna to the Son of David! If anyone is holy, let him come; if anyone is not so, let him repent. Even so, Lord, come. Amen.[15]

Evening has come. After we sing another hymn and greet one another with the peace of Christ, we depart for our homes. We are renewed spiritually with a stronger commitment and greater faith through the message Peter brought to us.

41

————ꙮꙮꙮ————

RUFUS

A real sense of excitement is sweeping across the congregations here in Rome. The apostle Paul has written a letter to our congregations. Paul has written letters to other churches, but they have always been to congregations he has founded through his work as a missionary—the congregations in Galatia, Philippi, Corinth, Colossae, and Thessalonica, for example. But Paul has never been to Rome, although I know he wants to visit us. We understand he would like to travel here and then move on west, to Spain, to establish congregations there. Perhaps our congregations will help him on his westward mission.

Several individuals have made copies of Paul's letter so it can be distributed quickly to all the congregations in the city. It is a laborious process to copy the letter by hand. Andronicus and I have received the copy for our congregation and have been able to read it from beginning to end. We plan to summarize the letter for the people in worship this next Lord's Day. Then at our meetings in succeeding weeks, we will read and teach from different portions of the letter.

Paul's letter has a message that astonishes me. The letter is really a statement of his theology, his beliefs. It is so well written and so logically constructed. Paul opens his letter with a greeting and a prayer of thanksgiving. Then he gets right to the heart of his faith. He declares that he is not ashamed of the gospel because it is the power of God for the salvation of everyone who has faith, both Jew and Gentile. At that point he writes a sentence that is packed with meaning. I had to read it several times to try to understand what he really is saying. Paul writes that the righteousness of God is revealed through faith for faith, and he buttresses that statement by quoting a few words from Habakkuk.

When first I read those few words—"through faith, for faith"—I did not really grasp the full meaning of what Paul was saying. Andronicus and I discussed this phrase. Finally we came to the conclusion that what Paul means is that God is faithful to the promises he has made to believers; that is, God does not in any way go back on any of his promises. God's faithfulness is the very basis of the faith we believers have. We can count on what God has promised because God always is faithful to what he has said. Then, because God is faithful to his word, we believers may put all our faith and trust in God's promises. What an amazing insight Paul has; the righteousness of God is revealed through faith—that is, through God's faithfulness—for faith—that is, for our faith and trust in God. Andronicus asked me to speak about that at our service.

Andronicus will summarize the next section in which Paul writes about the sinfulness of the world. Paul makes the point that all people have sinned, both Jew and Gentile, and he points out particularly to us Jews that the Law cannot save us. The Law can tell us what is right and what is wrong, but it has no power to give us the assurance of God's salvation. We Jews have sinned just as Gentiles have, so no one can stand in God's presence and claim to be righteous. Then he produces another one of those awesome statements. Paul writes that the only way we can be made righteous before God is through the gift of God's grace, the grace that is available for us through Jesus Christ.

I say I would like to speak to the congregation about the three images Paul uses to illustrate the grace of God given to us in Jesus Christ. He writes first that we believers are justified. This is an image from the judicial system. We have appeared in court before God, our judge, and he has ruled that we are free to go because our offenses have been forgiven. Then he writes that we are redeemed, an image from the slave markets. As slaves to sin, someone has paid the price of our redemption, and we are now free, no longer slaves to sin and guilt.

The third image is from the sacrificial rituals. We have had a sacrifice offered for our atonement. Christ has become the sacrificial lamb that sets us free from sin. The crucifixion that so troubled my father is the redemptive act God used to show his great love for us. All three of these images point to the same truth: those of us who believe are set free from the power of sin and guilt. We are forgiven.

Andronicus agrees to present the next section of the letter that tells about the hope and peace we have because of what Jesus Christ has done for us. Paul writes that since we are justified, that is, since we are forgiven, we have peace with God through our Lord Jesus Christ. He says that one man's disobedience, that is, Adam's sin, brought sin and death into our human experience while another man's act of righteousness, that is, Christ's death and resurrection, has opened the way for forgiveness and life to all people. In Christ every barrier to fellowship with God that is created by our sin and guilt is removed, and we are at peace with God.

I say I want to sum up the next section of Paul's letter. Here Paul writes that all things work together for good for those who love God. God works in all events in our lives, whether they are good or bad, to bring some good result. I have seen this happen. When my father was killed by the stallion, God used that event, terrible as it was, to bring Gaius and Julia and Olivia to faith in our Lord. Through their faith, other Gentiles in Cyrene have come to believe in Christ. Right after that insight, Paul affirms the faith we have as Christians in the most powerful confession of Christian faith I have ever heard.

> What then are we to say about these things? If God is for us, who is against us? He who did not withhold his own Son, but gave him up for all of us, will he not with him also give us everything else? Who will bring any charge against God's elect? It is God who justifies. Who is to condemn? It is Christ Jesus, who died, yes, who was raised, who is at the right hand of God, who indeed intercedes for us. Who will separate us from the love of Christ? Will hardship, or distress, or persecution, or famine, or nakedness, or peril, or sword? As it is written, 'For your sake we are being killed all day

long; we are accounted as sheep to be slaughtered.' No, in all these things we are more than conquerors through him who loved us. For I am convinced that neither death, nor life, nor angels, nor rulers, nor things present, nor things to come, nor powers, nor height, nor depth, nor anything else in all creation, will be able to separate us from the love of God in Christ Jesus our Lord.[16]

When I read those words, I know I can face anything with the faith and confidence that God will save me.

Andronicus takes the next section of the letter in which Paul writes about the great sorrow he feels because not all Jews have acknowledged Jesus as the Messiah. But he goes on to affirm his conviction that God will be gracious to the Jews. After all, God made a promise to the Jews that they would be his people, and God will not go back on that promise. If God were to renege on that promise, then we could not have faith in any of the promises God has made. God is righteous; God does what is right. God is faithful; God follows through on all the commitments he has made.

Paul then gives us some very practical guidance in how we should live as Christians. We are not to conform to the ways of the world; through repentance we are to be transformed in our thinking, in our opinions, and in our behavior. We are not to think of ourselves more highly than others because that kind of thinking lies at the very heart of human divisions. Paul says we are to be subject to the governing authorities because God has put them in place to keep order in society. We are not to judge one another but are to respect the opinions and beliefs concerning food and holy days that other people may observe. Above all else, we are not to do anything that will cause other believers to stumble in their beliefs or in their moral behavior.

At the close of the letter, Paul sends his greetings to the people he knows in Rome. He mentions Mother and me and names Junia and Andronicus, along with all the other leaders in our congregations in Rome.

Andronicus and I now know how we will present what Paul has written during our worship this Lord's Day. I am afraid our presentation will be rather long, but I know the people in our congregations want to hear what Paul has said. We all have heard of his great work as a missionary. Now we can learn from him what faith in Jesus Christ really means.

42

———◦◦◦◦◦◦◦◦———

ANDRONICUS

Junia and I invited Rufus, Suzanna, Miriam, and the girls for a meal at our home to meet Priscilla and Aquila, who went to Corinth when Emperor Claudius ordered all Jews to leave Rome. Priscilla and Aquila spent about a year and a half working with Paul in Corinth. Since we have received this letter from Paul, I believe it is important that we learn more about this remarkable Christian leader. After we greet one another and finish our meal I ask Aquila what he would like to share with us about Paul.

"Paul is a remarkable man. When the Jews were expelled from Rome twelve years ago, Priscilla and I went to Corinth, and it was there that we met Paul for the first time. He is a brilliant man. He grew up in Tarsus, a university town, and from an early age he was taught Greek learning and philosophy. He is well versed in Greek culture. Then he went to Jerusalem to study with Gamaliel, one of our foremost scholars. He was preparing to be a scholar and a rabbi."

"I can attest to his intellect," interjects Mother. "I knew him when I was in Antioch, and his skill as a teacher was very apparent to me. He could take a complex subject and make it clear to all of us. He is a very personable man as well."

At this point Priscilla recounts the story of Paul's conversion. "Paul persecuted believers in Christ. He was present when Stephen, our first martyr, was stoned to death. Shortly after that he went to Damascus to seize the believers there and bring them back to Jerusalem to be imprisoned. On the way, the risen Christ appeared to him and asked him why he was persecuting his followers. In that moment, Paul's life was changed. He became a witness for the very one whose followers he had been persecuting, and right after that he began to preach about Christ."

"Yes, Miriam says, "fifteen years ago Rufus and I were in Antioch when Paul and Barnabas started on the missionary journey they made to Cyprus and Galatia. They spent six years working with converts there."

Aquila picks up the conversation. "They worked primarily in four cities: Pisidian Antioch, Iconium, Lystra, and Derbe, establishing strong congregations there. It was too bad the team of Barnabas and Paul broke up after the council at Jerusalem. They worked so well together. But you know, God works in mysterious ways. Barnabas and Mark went off to Cyprus, and then Mark went on to Alexandria to work with Christians there. Paul and Silas visited the congregations that are in Galatia, and then they went on to Philippi, Thessalonica, Beroea, Athens, and Corinth, where Priscilla and I first met him. What a great privilege it was to assist Paul in establishing a strong Christian presence in that city. Later the Christians in Corinth became a source of anguish for Paul, but that is another story altogether. Paul also worked in Cenchreae, the seaport near Corinth. Phoebe, who is a member of another congregation here in Rome, was a deacon in the church Paul established there."

Priscilla then adds, "When Paul left Corinth, he took Aquila and me with him to Ephesus. Then he went on to Antioch. While we were in Ephesus, Apollos came there from Alexandria. Apollos is a very gifted leader who believed God was calling him to go to Corinth to work with the Christians there. We gave him some counsel, particularly teaching him about the work of the Holy Spirit, before he departed for Corinth."

Aquila, continuing the narrative, says, "Paul stayed only a short time in Antioch and then set off again on another journey. This time he visited those same congregations in Galatia and then traveled to Ephesus. He stayed there for three years; part of that time he spent in prison. From prison he sent letters to some of the churches he founded—the congregations in Philippi, Colossae, and Galatia. After Paul left Ephesus, he went on to visit the churches in Macedonia before returning to Jerusalem."

"I understand he should never have gone to Jerusalem," Andronicus remarks.

"His friends vigorously opposed his plan to go to Jerusalem, but Paul is a headstrong person. He rejected that advice. He barely escaped from Jerusalem with his life, and now he is being held captive in Caesarea," Aquila says.

"I understand that Paul wants to come to Rome. Is it his intention to use Rome as a base to expand his travels west to Spain?" asks Rufus.

"I believe it is," answers Priscilla, "and knowing Paul, as Aquila and I do, he will get here one way or another."

43

MIRIAM

J oseph has arrived on his voyage to Rome to deliver more of his horses to the army stationed here. Every time he comes, I get the urge to return to Cyrene with him. I have been in Rome nearly five years. It is an exciting place to be. I have come to know so many faithful leaders—Peter, Priscilla and Aquila, Andronicus and Junia. The fellowship we have enjoyed in our congregation has really strengthened my faith.

But I miss my family and friends in Cyrene. I have talked with Rufus and Suzanna about returning home, and they said they understand my desire to return to Cyrene. They also said I should go back with Joseph when he leaves Rome this year. Naomi and Mary are now six and four, and it is much easier for Suzanna to care for them. She really doesn't need my help the way she did a few years ago. I have other grandchildren in Cyrene, and I would like to see them.

I long for the calmer pace of life in Cyrene too. I'm not getting any younger, and I want to be able to slow down a bit. Life in Cyrene is so much easier than life in Rome. Joseph arrived today, and he is happy to have me accompany him on his journey back home.

I've asked Joseph to spend a few more days in Rome than he had planned so we may attend worship on the next Lord's Day. I want to have the opportunity to say good-bye to my wonderful friends in Rome, and I want to say farewell to Priscilla and Aquila too. By the middle of the week, Joseph and I will start down the road to Ostia to board a ship to Cyrene.

Of course, I will miss the girls and Rufus and Suzanna. I have grown so very fond of them. Suzanna has become the daughter I never had. I am torn, but at the same time I have made up my mind. It is time to go home.

I have been very fortunate. Very few women my age have had the opportunity to live in two important cities like Antioch and Rome. It has been exciting, and I have met so many important and wonderful people. But home is where my heart is, and home is where I shall go. I hope Rufus and Suzanna and the girls soon will follow. I know Jonathan has high hopes that Rufus will come back to lead our congregation in Cyrene. "'Til we meet again," I have said to them. "God be with you 'til we meet again."

44

—⎯ᨑᨏ•ᦢᨳᦢ•ᦢᨳᨎᦢᨏᨑ⎯—

ANDRONICUS

N ews travels fast these days. Paul is coming to Rome. He went to Jerusalem against the advice of people who were with him, and while he was there at the time of the festival of Pentecost, a group of men plotted to kill him. The danger was so great that a whole cohort of soldiers spirited him out of Jerusalem under the cover of darkness to take him to Caesarea. The authorities there detained him in prison for trial on charges that he was an agitator among the Jews and a leader in the sect of the Nazarene. He was held for two years while he awaited the disposition of these charges. Finally, under the rights Paul has as a Roman citizen, he appealed his case to the emperor in Rome. The ship that was carrying him to our city left port last fall. That ship ran into storms and was shipwrecked on Malta. Now we understand they have resumed their journey on another ship and should arrive in Rome very soon.

The Christians here in Rome are so excited by the news that Paul is coming. He has many friends here, and the letter he wrote to us has so impressed people that we cannot wait to hear from his own lips the testimony he has concerning his faith in Christ.

Some of the letters he has written to other churches have been transcribed and are being circulated among different churches in the empire. We are reading portions of them in our worship and are discussing what his words mean for us Christians.

As a church leader, I have been particularly interested in what he has written in comparing the church to the human body. The human body has many different parts—hands, feet, eyes, and ears. Each body part has its own function, and one part cannot say to another that it does not need that part. So it is with the church, the body of Christ, wrote Paul. There are different people who have different gifts from the Holy Spirit, and each person uses the gift God has given so the church may fulfill its mission in the world. Some people are apostles, like Junia and me; we can testify that we have seen the risen Christ. Others are prophets. Some are teachers, like Rufus, and there are people who have the gift of healing. Some are good at administration. Others are natural leaders, and some people speak in tongues. The people who have all these different gifts from the Spirit operate together to do the work Christ has given to his church.

What Junia finds more attractive, however, is the greater gift Paul writes about, the gift of love. What he says is so profound and so true.

> Love is patient; love is kind; love is not envious or boastful or arrogant or rude. It does not insist on its own way; it is not irritable or resentful; it does not rejoice in wrongdoing, but rejoices in the truth. It bears all things, believes all things, hopes all things, endures all things. Love never ends.[17]

Whatever particular gift we may have, all of us need the gift of love. That is what holds us together and makes it possible for us to serve Christ. There are faith, hope, and love, writes Paul, but the greatest of these is love. How true! If we don't love one another, we really cannot do the work of Christ.

God has set the example for us. God loves us so much that he sent his Son into the world so we who believe in him may have life that is abundant and eternal. Because God loves us, we know he does not condemn us but saves us. Finally, because God loves us we are to love one another.

45

———⁓⚬⊙⚬⊙⚬⊙⚬⊙⚬⊙⚬⊙⚬⁓———

RUFUS

Almost six months have passed since Paul arrived in Rome. He has been living under house arrest just outside the city. There are soldiers who constantly guard him. Paul cannot move about freely, but there are no restrictions on who may visit him. Many of the church leaders here in Rome have met with him. People from all over the city and the nearby countryside come to learn from Paul and hear his testimony concerning his convictions about belief in Christ.

I have gone with other church leaders to listen to Paul speak about Christian faith, but today I have an opportunity to join a small group who will meet with Paul. This will give me a chance to ask him some questions that have been churning in my mind. Andronicus, Junia, Priscilla, and Aquila are joining me in this meeting.

When we arrive at the house where Paul is staying, he greets each one of us and then immediately begins to reminisce with Priscilla and Aquila about the time they spent together in Corinth.

"It really was one of the wonderful blessings that come from God that brought us together in Corinth. I know it was difficult for you to leave your home in Rome when Claudius ordered all the Jews to leave the capital, but I see God's hand in that edict preparing the way for the three of us to meet in Corinth to work together in establishing the congregation there."

"We had a very profitable ministry," responds Aquila. "That congregation has become one of the very strong Christian communities in the Greek world."

"Oh, yes," adds Priscilla. "But it was not accomplished without a real struggle, was it, Paul? For a while I thought that congregation was going to reject completely your leadership."

"Well I had to take a stand against those people in the church who were involved in acts of sexual immorality," explains Paul. "The elders there would not excommunicate the guilty parties and their sins were corrupting the morals of the whole congregation. I wrote that sharp letter criticizing them for accepting the gross behavior of those few people who would not change their ways and live as Christ commands. But my blunt criticism did have a positive effect. They wrote back later to say they respected me and were sorry they had not taken my advice when I first offered it."

I am beginning to feel like the neglected partner in this meeting, but then Paul turns to me. "Rufus, I remember some of the things your mother said about your father's carrying the cross of Jesus when she was in Antioch, but what was it that brought him to the point of believing in Jesus?"

"That whole experience in Jerusalem the day after Passover was distressing for Father" I begin. "When he came home he could not talk about what he had seen, even with Mother. He was convinced Jesus was innocent of any wrong and the injustice and cruelty of the crucifixion troubled him deeply. Fortunately he had crops that had to be harvested and that work kept his mind off what he had seen. After several weeks he began to talk with us about his experiences, but it was not until Lucius, Daniel, and Jonathan returned and told him what had happened at Pentecost that he really had a sense of peace about the crucifixion. When they said Jesus had been resurrected from the dead and he came to believe that himself, he could see the plan God had for us. He was a firm believer in Jesus. After that stallion trampled him and he was at the point of death, to see his eyes light up as he took Jesus' hand and went to be with him in heaven was truly a witness to faith that will stay with me until the day I die."

"Tell me a little more about that vision he had," said Paul.

"We knew Father was dying; there was no way he could recover from his wounds. He appeared to be in a coma and his breathing was becoming more labored and sporadic. The whole congregation was in our home and we all just expected him to slip away. But at the last moment Father opened his eyes and looked toward the ceiling. He lifted his right arm and stretched out his hand, and said, 'It's Jesus, the man whose cross I carried. He is reaching out his hand to take me with him into his kingdom.' That confirmed for all of us the victory Jesus has won for us over death."

The room was quiet for a few moments.

Paul broke the silence, "I remember your mother's telling that story to the congregation in Antioch. They were encouraged by what she said. Is your mother still here in Rome?"

"No, she went back to Cyrene nearly two years ago. From what I hear she is doing well. I am sure she wishes she could see you again, Paul."

"Some day we will meet again, Rufus. All of us will be together again when we are united with Christ in his kingdom."

At this point I have Paul's full attention so I decide to ask him the questions I have been wanting to ask.

"Paul," I ask, "I have studied what you wrote in several of your letters, particularly the one you wrote to us Christians here in Rome. I would like to hear more about your teachings concerning the Holy Spirit. Just how does the Holy Spirit work in our lives?"

"Well, Rufus, when Jesus met with his disciples in the Upper Room just before he was crucified, he promised the Holy Spirit would come to them to take his place in their lives. The Holy Spirit would remind them of all the things Jesus had said when he was on earth. The Holy Spirit would be their helper and their advocate. The Holy Spirit would guide them and show them what they should do as God's faithful servants.

"Then on the day of Pentecost, the Holy Spirit came upon the disciples with a display of great power, and all kinds of amazing things began to happen. Many people were converted. Healings occurred. The Holy Spirit gave the followers of Jesus power to testify to the truth Jesus came to proclaim. I personally saw this when Stephen, a deacon of the church, was stoned to death. He declared with great courage and conviction that Jesus is the Messiah, and as he lay dying, he forgave those who were throwing the stones that killed him. Then as I persecuted Christians in Jerusalem, I saw their determination to follow Jesus to the point of personal harm, imprisonment, and even death. It was the Holy Spirit who gave them the courage to be true to their beliefs.

"When the risen Christ appeared to me on the road to Damascus, the Holy Spirit led me into the city and guided Ananias to come to me. Ananias didn't want to come. He believed I might have faked a conversion to get inside the church at Damascus to destroy it. The Holy Spirit compelled him to come. The Holy Spirit then began to guide me and help me become a true follower of Christ. The Holy Spirit is the person God gives to help us understand the truth that Jesus came to reveal. The Spirit guides us so we may live according to that truth and encourages us to believe with our whole minds and hearts the truth that comes from God. The Holy Spirit is God who is with us every moment of every day that we live, guiding, supporting, and encouraging us in our faith."

"I think I understand that. But I am wondering if you can say a little more about what you wrote in the letter you sent to our church here in Rome. I'm not sure I can quote you exactly, but you wrote something about people walking in the way of the flesh when they set their minds on the things of the flesh. But we Christians are to set our minds on the things of the Spirit so we may walk in the way of the Spirit. What do you mean by flesh and Spirit? Does flesh simply refer to our bodies? Certainly we cannot escape from our bodies before we die."

"Perhaps I should have made the meaning a little clearer. No, flesh is not really one's body. Flesh is our sinful human nature. In my letter to the congregations in Galatia, I tried to make that clear. What I wrote to them is that the works of the flesh, that is, the inclinations of our sinful human nature, are fornication, impurity, licentiousness, idolatry, sorcery, enmities, strife, jealousy, anger, quarrels, dissensions, factions, envy, drunkenness, carousing, and things like these. As human beings, we are tempted to do all of these things, and all of these sins, when we give in to them, create problems in our human society. On the other hand, when we are guided by the Holy Spirit, we will show love, joy, peace, patience, kindness, generosity, faithfulness, gentleness, and self-control. The Holy Spirit working in our lives guides us and enables us to resist the temptations of our sinful human nature, what I call flesh. Then the Holy Spirit helps us to display in our lives those characteristics that I label the fruits of the Spirit. When we display these characteristics, we do what is constructive in human affairs. Does that make sense to you?"

"Yes it does. Let me see if I can state in a few sentences what I have heard you say, Paul. The Holy Spirit is the person God sends to keep Jesus' teachings alive in our minds and hearts. The Holy Spirit gives us the courage of our Christian convictions so we may provide an effective witness for Christ. And the Holy Spirit gives us the strength to resist the temptations of our sinful human nature so we may display love, joy, peace, and all of those other characteristics Christ wants us to show in our lives."

"I think you understand now how the Holy Spirit works in the lives of all believers," says Paul. "We are continually tempted to do what is wrong. The Holy Spirit helps us do what is right, what Christ would have us do."

Paul then turns back to Andronicus and asks, "Is this the promising young man you told me about whom you are grooming to be a pastor in the church?"

"This is he," Andronicus replies.

I guess that sinful human nature gets hold of me in that moment, because suddenly I am filled with pride.

46

━━∽〜⌒〇⌒〇⌒〜∽━━

SUZANNA

Rufus and I have lived in Rome for nine years now. It has been a great adventure, and both of us have learned so much about our Christian faith. We have benefited from our contacts with Aquila and Priscilla, Peter, Paul, John Mark, and Andronicus and Junia. But I am beginning to feel a desire to go back to Cyrene. I have not seen my parents for nine years, and they have never seen Mary and have not seen Naomi since she was very young. I have good friends in our church here, but I remember good friends in Cyrene too. City life is exciting, but it can become a little too hectic. And I would like to have our daughters experience the kind of life Rufus and I had in our hometown.

We have a routine here. Rufus enjoys teaching. Both Naomi and Mary go with him to attend his classes. It's hard for me to believe how fast the girls are growing. Naomi is ten, and Mary is eight. Rufus says both girls are very intelligent, and Mary particularly pursues learning with a real passion. I think that is her nature. I have always believed she will make her mark in the world. It is the fact that our girls are growing up that gives me a greater desire to return home. They should have contact with family members in Cyrene as they mature. I have always hoped they would marry someone from our hometown rather than someone here in Rome. I want them to experience what life is like in a smaller community with a more rural lifestyle.

This morning after Rufus and the girls leave for school, I go to the market, as I usually do. I hear some gossip there that I must discuss with Rufus. It is troubling. It involves our emperor, Nero. I usually don't pay attention to what people say about political matters, but for some reason, this really catches my attention. Perhaps I latch onto it because it may be a sign of some difficulty for us in Rome, and if Rufus agrees with me, he may be more inclined to leave behind our life in this city.

When Rufus returns from teaching and we eat our meal, the two of us have a chance to talk.

"Rufus, I overheard two women talking about our emperor when I was at the market this morning. They are slaves in the household of a member of the senate. The senators apparently are very concerned about the stability of our emperor and the effect his actions may have on his governing decisions.

"They said that until last year, Emperor Nero had two faithful advisors, Burrus and Seneca. These two men restrained Nero from some of the excesses he apparently wanted to pursue. Their advice has been very beneficial for the people in Rome, and they have prevented our emperor from making decisions that might harm the citizens of the empire. But last year Burrus died, and Nero appointed a man named Tigellinus to replace him.

"Seneca could not bear working with Tigellinus; they clashed all the time on policy decisions. The advice one gave was at odds with the advice the other gave, and Nero seemed to favor the advice Tigellinus gave. Seneca finally resigned in frustration. Tigellinus is a corrupt man, and he has been giving Nero advice to pursue excesses, orgies, and even murder. After Seneca resigned and Tigellinus became his only advisor, Nero divorced Octavia on a trumped-up charge of adultery and then had her murdered. Free of his ties to Octavia, he married his longtime mistress, Poppaea Sabina."

"We have heard all of this before, Suzanna, and while Emperor Nero's actions are reprehensible, they have not really harmed the empire," Rufus replied.

"That is true, Rufus, but these two women today added some new information to what we have previously heard. Nero has apparently been involved in a number of orgies, and he has been interested in performing on the stage, singing and accompanying himself on the lyre. Until recently he has done that only in private gatherings. Last year, however, he went to Naples to perform on the stage.

"The senators opposed this performance. They believe it is unseemly for the emperor to perform on the stage, and they are morally outraged concerning some of the other things Nero has done. Following his appearance in Naples, an earthquake destroyed the stage on which Nero had performed, and the people have taken that as a bad omen. Now Nero has returned to Naples to perform again, and the senators are absolutely opposed to his behavior.

"This may seem like a small thing, but it shows the emperor and the senate are at odds with one another, and Emperor Nero is not getting good advice from Tigellinus. I think it could be only a short time before something terrible may happen here in Rome."

"Are you sure, Suzanna, that these people you talked with are telling the truth about what is going on in our government?"

"Well, I have no way of verifying these facts, but these women seem to be reporting accurately what they have heard. As servants of a senator, they are in a position to eavesdrop and overhear conversations other people do not hear. They are Christians, too, members of another congregation in the city, and I have no reason to doubt their word. They are very concerned, and they say the senators are really troubled by these developments.

"When Nero began as our emperor, he seemed to be making good decisions, like rescinding Claudius's rule expelling all Jews from Rome. But now he is going against the opinions of the senators, and certainly that is not good for the citizens of Rome. He appears to be making harmful decisions, like divorcing his wife and then having her murdered so he could marry his mistress. That is truly evil. His orgies may indicate he is mentally unstable. Then this business of performing on a stage, singing and playing his lyre, just seems out of place for an emperor."

"If these reports are true, I am troubled as well. It may be time for us to consider returning home to Cyrene. Corruption like this in the government can weaken the rule of law in the empire. Cyrene is still a part of the empire, but at least we would be away from the center of power and corruption."

"We have a good life here in Rome, Rufus, and you love your work teaching the children and assisting Andronicus in the pastoral work in our congregation. I am torn. I enjoy our relationship with the people here, but I miss Cyrene and our family and friends there."

"I feel a sense of commitment to be here to help Andronicus and Junia. But my move to Rome was supposed to be temporary to meet Christian leaders here and learn from them. My true mission is to be a pastor in Cyrene. Perhaps we should start planning to go back home."

"I certainly would support that decision. Will you speak to Andronicus and Junia about our plan to return home?"

"Yes, I'll tell them that after I have completed my teaching responsibilities this summer, we plan to return to Cyrene. I'm sure they will agree that is the right thing for us to do. They understand that our move to Rome was to be temporary. They may not want us to go, but I believe they will see it is right for us to go home. The people in Cyrene will certainly be very happy to have us return. It really seems that God is leading us back to Cyrene to fulfill our mission there."

47

―⁓⟊⟋⊙⟊⊙⟊⟋⊙⟊⁓―

RUFUS

I t started as a glow in the eastern sky on the eighteenth day of the month. A dangerous fire began to sweep across the city of Rome. The fire burned for six days. Three of the fourteen districts in Rome were completely destroyed, and seven other districts, including the one where we lived, were badly damaged. Only four districts have not been touched by the flames. As the fire spread, people fled from their homes ahead of the conflagration.

Many people have lost their homes and all their possessions. Suzanna, our girls, and I are among them. Our apartment building burned to the ground. We are homeless, but we are very fortunate. Andronicus and Junia's home is in one of the four districts that has no damage. In an act of Christian charity, they have opened their home to our family and the other families of the congregation whose apartments were destroyed. Those of us who are homeless are living in their courtyard. The girls enjoy sleeping under the stars, but we know this cannot be a permanent situation for our family. We thank God no one in our congregation died in the fire and that we have a place to stay.

The next morning as Andronicus and Junia make their way around their courtyard checking with each family to be certain they are doing well, they come to the small space where our family is located. I had talked with Andronicus and Junia about our family returning to Cyrene before this fire began, and as I expected, they reluctantly agreed with our decision. Now that the fire has destroyed our home, Suzanna and I have decided to advance the date of our departure.

"Andronicus and Junia," I begin, "thank you so much for opening your home for all of us to stay here. As you know Suzanna and I have decided to leave Rome and now that our home has been destroyed in the fire we have talked about advancing the date of our departure and leaving as soon as we can arrange passage on a ship in Ostia. We plan to go to the seaport today to see if there is a ship leaving soon for Cyrene."

"Well Junia and I understand why you would want to leave now. I wonder, Rufus, if you would be willing to stay for several months to help the families that are here find new homes. There is so much work to be done. Would you mind, Suzanna, if your husband stayed behind for several months while we help all these people find new homes?"

"No, if Rufus wants to stay I will be willing to have him do that. I can see there is much to be done and I know you can use all the help you can get. Are you agreeable, Rufus?"

"Yes, of course I am."

"Fine," says Andronicus, "I won't keep him here any longer than is necessary, Suzanna. I know you don't want to be separated very long."

With that Andronicus and Junia move on to check with the family next to us. Suzanna, I, and the girls gather our few possessions and set out for Ostia. That evening our good fortune continues. We contact Philip and his family, where we stayed nine years ago when we arrived from Cyrene, and they are more than generous in providing a place for us while we try to locate a ship crossing the sea. We are not the only people leaving Rome. Others are going back to their home provinces now that the fire has destroyed large parts of the city. Finally I locate a ship traveling to Cyrene. We go to the dock early in the morning, and I bid a tearful farewell to Suzanna and our girls.

I hold Naomi and Mary close and kiss them. Then I embrace Suzanna for as long as I can before she and the girls have to board the ship. I promise I will follow them in a few short months. Suzanna acts as if she wants to tell me something, but then she turns away, takes the girls' hands, and walks up the gangway. They stand at the rail and wave. As the ship drifts away from the dock, we keep waving to one another.

I hurry from the dock and run back to Ostia to stand on the shore, waiting for the ship to pass. With sails unfurled and filled with air, the ship moves down the coast toward the open sea. We watch and wave until the ship is out of sight.

Then with a heavy heart I turn to walk back to Rome to take up the work of rebuilding and restoring homes for the people of our congregation.

48

───wwvw∘◦╰◉╯◦∘wwvw───

ANDRONICUS

Rumors have begun to circulate among the people in Rome that we Christians are responsible for starting the fire that ravaged our city. The emperor apparently is the one spreading this report. We are not sure where Nero was when the fire started, but when the flames were extinguished, he opened his palace to house some of the homeless people in the city.

However, soon after the fire was extinguished, the people in Rome began to wonder if Nero started the fire. They know Nero wants to rebuild the city, making it more beautiful and renewing areas like Subura that are blighted. People began to jump to the conclusion that the fire was the first step in Nero's renewal program, so in the last two months many people have blamed the emperor for starting the fire. They are angry. They have lost their homes and their possessions. They are losing faith in the emperor too.

Now Nero is striking back with a publicity campaign to deflect the blame for this fire. Realizing he needs to find a scapegoat for the destruction, he has circulated the report that we Christians set the city ablaze. He is enhancing the story to increase the people's anger at us by saying we are cannibals who eat the body and drink the blood of our Lord in our worship. These accusations are ridiculous, but the people are beginning to believe we are the ones to blame for the fire that destroyed their homes. I don't know how we can rebut this report.

The tide of public opinion is turning against us, and we have no way to counter these false reports. We are powerless. All the power is in the hands of Nero and the officials in the government. We are at their mercy.

On the Lord's Day, our congregation gathers for worship as we normally do. Rufus and I are leading the worship that day. We chant a psalm, and then Rufus begins our service with a prayer. He uses the model prayer Jesus taught his disciples.

> Our Father in heaven, your name is holy. May your kingdom come and your will be done on earth as it is in heaven. Give us this day our daily bread. Forgive our sins as we forgive others who sin against us. Lead us not into temptation, but deliver us from evil. Amen.

Then I take a loaf of bread and break it, saying, "This is the body of Christ; take and eat."

At that point, eight or ten soldiers break down the door to our home, and brandishing their swords and spears, they interrupt our worship by loudly shouting, "Seize the cannibals who eat the body and drink the blood of this Jesus! Arrest these infidels, these traitors who have set fire to our city!"

We all recoil in fear. Two soldiers come forward, roughly grab Rufus and me by the arms, and throw us to the ground. They hold spears against our necks. The other soldiers seize eight or ten men in the congregation. The women and children scream and cry. No one makes any move to resist the soldiers. We all realize that would be futile. We have no weapons. The power of the empire is stacked against us.

After the soldiers have rounded up some men from our congregation, they pull Rufus and me to our feet. They tie our hands behind us and push us out of our home, forcing us to walk to a makeshift prison near the Forum. We do not know what our fate will be. We earnestly pray God will deliver us from the hands of the soldiers, but soon we realize that is not to be.

After we arrive at our prison, we learn that similar raids have been conducted against many other congregations in the city. Dozens upon dozens of us Christians are being held on charges that are complete fabrications. We did not set fire to the city, and we certainly are not cannibals. But we can do nothing; there is nothing, absolutely nothing, we can do to escape our fate.

The next day we learn how we will die. Three methods of torture and death are being used: crucifixion, facing wild animals the Coliseum, and in the evening being tied to a pole and set on fire to give light to the area around the forum. None of us knows how we will die; we only know death is imminent. We do not want to die, but each one of us is firm in his resolve not to escape death by denying our faith in Christ. We will be faithful to the end.

In the first two days we are imprisoned, different ones of us are taken off to suffer a terrible death, and each day more and more of our brothers in Christ join us in prison. Rufus and I and the men in our congregation spend many hours in prayer. People from other congregations either create their own group for spiritual strength or join a group that has already formed. We console one another and encourage each other to maintain a strong faith and commitment to our risen Lord.

Four nights after we were arrested, a soldier comes to our area of the prison and singles out Rufus, ordering him to come.

I quickly embrace him and whisper, "The Lord be with you."

He responds, "And with you."

Rufus then walks boldly with the cadre of solders. He is taken from our fellowship. We join in prayer for him. Both he and we know what will happen. Rufus will be tied to a pole and set on fire to provide light for people walking at night along the Forum. It is a horrible way to die but perhaps no worse than being torn apart by wild animals or fastened to a cross. We pray that God will be with Rufus to give him courage to be faithful to Christ. We are confident God will give him the strength to bear the pain of death.

The next morning a sympathetic Roman soldier, who was so impressed by what he saw, tells us how Rufus died. As the soldiers bound Rufus to the pole, this soldier said, Rufus looked at them and prayed God would forgive them for what they were doing. Then he said, "Nothing can separate me from the love of God as it is found in

Jesus Christ; not death, not anything." When the fire was set, Rufus lifted his eyes heavenward, and as the flames ignited his clothing, he uttered one word, "Father . . ." and then he gave up his spirit to Almighty God.

EPILOGUE

Suzanna's labor continues for thirteen hours, more than twice as long as the labor she endured with her girls. Her mother and Mother Miriam are with her through the birthing process. When the baby finally appears, he gives out a lusty cry. Suzanna's mother ties the umbilical cord and cuts it. Mother Miriam cleans up the baby and gives him to Suzanna. The completely exhausted mother clasps her baby to her breast, and the infant's crying stops.

Suzanna's mother goes to the door to tell her husband he should come into the room. "It's a boy," she announces.

"My dear daughter, congratulations on the birth of your son," says Jonathan. Then he notices the tears forming in Suzanna's eyes and rolling down her cheeks. "Why are you crying?" he asks. "This is a time for rejoicing."

"I am so sorry Rufus is not here, and I so wish I had told him as I left Ostia that I was pregnant. I almost told him, but I wasn't completely certain I was pregnant, and I didn't want to give him false hope that we would have another child. I assumed that he would come to me in Cyrene in a few short months. I wanted to surprise him with the news when he arrived. Now he will never know he has a son."

"Oh, he knows, Suzanna; Rufus knows. Are you going to name your son Rufus for his father?"

"No, when I was pregnant with the girls, Rufus and I decided that if we had a son we would name him Simon Christopher—Simon for his grandfather and Christopher, which, as you know means Christ-bearer, the one who bears Christ in his soul. Both names are in honor of Rufus's father."

"What an excellent name for such a wonderful little boy! I am certain that is a name he will live up to. Simon Christopher will do great things for Christ!"

And the cross-bearer's legacy continues . . .

ENDNOTES

1   Psalm 24:3-8
2   Psalm 24:9-10
3   Deuteronomy 6:4-5
4   Deuteronomy 28:12
5   Psalm 122:1-4.
6   Psalm 121:1-8.
7   Zechariah 9:9.
8   Psalm 116:1-5.
9   Deuteronomy 26:5b-9
10 Psalm 116:12-18.
11 Acts 15:23-29
12 Philippians 2:5-11.
13 *The Didache*, chapter 9.
14 Ibid.
15 *The Didache*, chapter 10.
16 Romans 8:31-39.
17 1 Corinthians 13:4-8a.

CPSIA information can be obtained at www.ICGtesting.com
Printed in the USA
BVOW04s1631190813

328870BV00001B/1/P